SOLID

BROKEN

CHANGING

SOLID

BROKEN

CHANGING

Elizabeth Ellsworth

Dragon Tail Books
Brooklyn, New York
Provincetown, MA

Dragon Tail Books
Brooklyn, New York
Provincetown, MA

for JEK
and JK, DK, MK
wayfinders, one and all

CONTENTS

"On the days of their demise, reinventing themselves with the dedication of a bird sitting on eggs, things shed skins. That's how it is…what could there be to regret? …things move on by shedding skins. And so, setting forth will bring good fortune indeed. How could you ever go astray?"

Hexagram 49 "SHEDDING SKIN"
from *I Ching: The Book of Change*
Translation by David Hinton

BEFORE EVERYTHING CHANGED (BEC)

 on the last day, BEC (Before Everything Changed).

The calm, late summer waters. The glittery morning sunlight. Dad, fine tuning the rudder in that vigilant way of his—which you would expect from a guy who just quit his big career in emergency management. Me, working the sail and not fully awake. Both of us, gross from camping on the boat last night.

But *Home*, our small and very handmade wooden boat, is looking the way she always does—fresh, like new, totally loved up.

I shake off my sleepiness enough to trim *Home*'s sail and fasten the mainsheet. With a slow yawn, I settle myself in the cockpit, snap open the clip on my gear bag and pull out my sketchbook.

I count on my drawings. They're signals, really, from the

only part of me that has any clue about—yeah—what's up with my life. They can be cryptic, and I'm used to that. But lately, I've been covering pages with jumbled scribbles— garbled messages about—I can't tell what. It's as if someone or some *thing* hacked into my sketchbook. Someone or something too messed up to make sense.

Thumbing through the drawings from the last few days is creeping me out. But I refuse to give up my hopes for this weekend, so I turn to a new page and dig through the gear bag for a marker. This is our last sail of the summer. In such a dazzling August dawn, how hard could it be, finally, to dream that dream? You know, the big future I'm supposed to be plotting a course for this year. My life's purpose. The reason the new high school I just moved to is taking us on that five-college tour next week.

In a flash of optimism, I pull myself out of my sleepy funk, address the blank expanse of the pages in front of me, and let my hand go.

A line flows from the marker, curving up and then down across both pages, repeating the pattern. When my hand slows to a stop, I lift the pen and lean back against *Home*'s rail. Holding my breath, I take a stab at making sense of what I see.

At least there's some order to it. At least it is not the tangled mess of yesterday's drawings. Still, the longer I look at what I have drawn, the tighter I grip the marker.

I can feel Dad studying me from the helm seat as if I'm an emergency about to happen. I didn't think it was that obvious. I shake out my cramped hand and force myself to refocus on the drawing. But just when I think I see something in the sweep of lines, whatever it might have been evaporates in the heat of Dad's worried stare.

I flash him a *what!?* look. But he dodges it and pretends to examine *Home*'s sail.

Now my neck is tight. Because I'm not the only emergency about to happen—he has been keeping something from me for days.

Whatever it is, I can't take it on right now. I'm under deadline. My drawings and I have three days to come up with a dream to take on that college tour.

Trying to ward off yet another bout of anxiety about big futures, *and* big family secrets, I release my shoulders and stretch my neck. Then, I look out across the bow at the dazzling water, and—yeah—at the last moments of life, BEC.

I snap awake. Something is coming. The sunlight, air, ocean—they feel like they're turning inside out.

My eyes flash to the lines I drew minutes ago. It's beyond obvious that they are waves—waves charging into and over one another. I sit bolt upright and scan the horizon for—I don't know what.

At that very moment, Dad decides he has finally mustered up the required energy to start that father-daughter conversation he should have started days ago.

"Kally, I've been thinking, this might be a good time to—"

"Come about." I gasp the words, like a person who is fighting to wake from a suffocating dream.

"What? Why?"

But I don't know what or why. I wish he could tell me what or why. As I turn from the sea to my dad, my eyes catch on what is forming behind him.

"What's wrong?" Dad twists in his seat to look behind him.

And now, we are both gaping into the maw of one insanely huge wave. It is bearing down on us. It is growing.

In his best emergency management voice, Dad orders me to "ready to come about."

I scramble to release the mainsheet. Dad shoves the rudder hard over. We duck. The boom and sail swing their long arc, grazing the tops of our heads. I give the sail a second to refill with air before I trim it and fasten the mainsheet.

Dad is steering us straight into the swelling bulge of ocean.

"Dad?"

"We're OK. We're good." I believe him because he's the world's best sailor. Then again, there is a heaving surge of Atlantic Ocean off of *Home*'s bow. It's charging at us. The closer it gets, the more vertical it becomes. Soon, it fills the whole world. We are at the foot of a gigantic ramp of blue-grey salt water gone solid.

The mass rises under *Home*. It propels us skyward. *Home* twists and bends in ten directions at once, giving off tortured creaks and groans.

My stomach bottoms out like it's in a violent high-speed elevator. The instant change of direction from forward to straight up spills all wind from our sail. It goes limp and pathetically useless.

I turn to make sure Dad is still inside the boat. He is. He's struggling to gain control of the rudder and stop *Home* from wiping out as the monster wave builds to its crest, suspends us endlessly at its peak—then drops.

Home skids down the backside of the surge.

I take a death grip on the cockpit rail. My ability to process what is happening stutters into slow motion. Before I can scream or do something more useful, the wave—if you can call it that—barrels on toward the horizon. In seconds, the surrounding sea flattens.

Home sways violently, then droops, stunned and wrung out. She was born in these waters. She knows them intimately. What they did just now is beyond comprehension. Given the reality warp that rolled through a minute ago, the calm we are sitting in is outrageous. Laughable, even.

I'm not laughing. I'm shaking. Because—yeah—one second, it's the most flawless morning ever for a late summer sail. And the next, it's a trailer for a preposterous disaster movie.

Except, what passed under us was no computer animation.

Barely able to think or speak, I croak: "Where did it come from?"

Even though his face is as white as *Home*'s sail, Dad is fully functional and already in response mode. He points to the rocky island off starboard. "We should steer close to East Ledge Island. Ready to come about."

I'm grateful for the call to do something within the realm of normal. Hands trembling, I rescue my sketchbook from the water sloshing at my feet, seal it in the dry bag and stow it in *Home*'s cabin. Returning to my position, I take hold of the mainsheet and try to sound ready when I say, "Ready."

Dad thrusts the rudder hard over. The mainsheet runs through my hands and the boom swings past our heads. I close my grip, trim sail, and fasten the line.

As we beat windward toward East Ledge Island, my body continues to vibrate on high alert. That must be why, when I spot the clouds that have appeared at the horizon, I literally shudder. Those clouds are…wrong.

Dad pushes a life jacket into my hands.

Home settles into a solid and steady course toward East Ledge Island. It's beyond me how she can do that after what she has been through, but it makes me love her more than ever.

The two humans on board are far from solid or steady. We do not speak about what just happened to us *or* the ocean, much less to the rules we thought our home planet was playing by. Dad has that look he gets when he is doing a situation assessment. And, like me, he keeps checking out those unrecognizable clouds behind us.

For my part, I'm awash in post-wave shock due to my inability to ignore how we almost died minutes ago. And, my alarm over the clouds that are closing in on us has just bumped up a level. At the rate they are moving, they'll be overhead before we make it to the island.

Fear pounds in my chest. The sky is about to behave as insanely as the ocean did. Meanwhile, wind speed at sea level keeps dropping. And that is unnerving in a whole other way.

I look to the small island that Dad is steering toward for some hint of reassurance.

The bronzed cliffs of East Ledge Island shoot up from the water, then turn rolling and grassy at their tops. A veteran lighthouse, East Ledge Light, sits dangerously close to the brink of its sandy perch.

I retrieve a dry bag from inside *Home*'s cockpit, pull out our binoculars, and scan the island's jagged outcroppings of rock. They jut out of the narrow beach in long lines before trailing into the ocean. Some of the boulders would dwarf a small house.

Looking for signs of people, I pan up the cliff, beyond a cluster of service buildings, and over to what must be the keeper's house. East Ledge seems to be as deserted as it is remote. According to the map we memorized for this trip, it's out here alone, 15.7 miles from the mainland.

I scan the binoculars down the wood stairs that connect the lighthouse grounds to a sandy cove. A twenty-foot long, high-speed aluminum workboat comes into view. It seesaws at a short wooden pier piled high with vacation gear worthy of the back of an oversized SUV. The pilot of the workboat unloads a boogie board and adds it to the line-up of coolers, duffels, grill, lawn chairs, and beach umbrellas.

That's when I spot him, the guy whose name—I am destined to learn before long—is Stuart. Granted, this is one of the more significant events of this, the day Everything Changes—but me glimpsing Stuart is *not* what "changes everything." He shows up as a mere blob in the binoculars, but he's an impressively athletic blob. He's grabbing assorted bags of vacation gear out of the workboat and swinging them up onto the pier in official naval maneuver fashion.

The man pacing the pier next to him, I am further destined to learn, is Mark Hart, Stuart's dad. He holds a cellphone up to the sky in doomed attempts to find a signal. The woman who is supervising the activities with an anxious energy that I'm picking up from way out here is Jennifer Hart, Stuart's mom.

Incoming waves slam into the back of the workboat and send it banging against the wooden pilings. Stuart makes a deft leap and pushes the boat clear.

At the end of the pier, Stuart's little sister, Ollie, takes pictures of the sky. She begins to gesture excitedly, and that makes me remember—

I lower my binoculars and look overhead. Those clouds are pumped up, boiling, and coming at us fast. But here at sea level, the wind has slackened even more. *Home* is making little headway in the long swells that are growing beneath her.

I swing the binoculars back to the island, but everyone there is too busy to notice us. Stuart struggles against the waves that are crashing the workboat into the ocean rowboat tied alongside it. Finally, he muscles the workboat free of the pier. The pilot guns the motor, steers north along the shoreline, and disappears around the curve of the island.

I watch Stuart take a cap from his back pocket and pull it over his buzz cut. His mother looks like she's shivering as she pulls her daughter to her side. Everyone grabs what they can carry and rushes up the steps to the top of the bluff.

When I lower the binoculars, I realize I'm shivering cold too. So is Dad. The temperature has gone from August to November in seconds. Surface winds have dropped to a dead calm. Still, the swells build. That line of clouds has morphed into squall cells, and they are writhing above us.

I stow the binoculars and break out our sweatshirts. We slip out of the lifejackets. Dad uses his knees to steady the rudder while he wrestles his sweatshirt on over his head. I zip up my hoodie and get back into position to work the mainsheet. Finally, we help each other back into our lifejackets and Dad breaks our nerve-wracked silence.

"Prepare to tack."

"Ready," I say.

Dad pushes the tiller to starboard. I haul in the mainsheet. The boom swings past our heads. Less than a minute later, he says again, "Prepare to tack." I let out the mainsheet and duck under the boom.

"The currents out here should push us toward the island, but we're getting nowhere," I say.

Beneath us, the sea is acting nothing like it's supposed to. Above us, the storm cells have tightened into raging, purple-black coils. Dad eyes the pier at East Ledge. I can tell he's calculating how to put in there, as if there's wind enough to put in anywhere.

"We'll make way for that beach below the lighthouse," he says, using his captain's voice. "We can rest up for a couple hours. Let this weather pass. Then, we'll head for home."

I'm about to ask if he had seen the people landing on the island few minutes ago. But then, things go from being merely beyond strange to being—yeah—whatever word you would grasp for to describe The Day Everything Changed.

The wind strengthens and veers. Dad wrestles with the rudder as *Home*'s sail whips in one direction and then snaps in another. I let out the mainsheet, haul it back in, and let it out again.

"It's coming from every direction. How can it even do that?" I shout, fighting the boom. Dad braces himself against the edge of the cockpit, trying to get more leverage on the tiller. Within seconds, we are fighting to stop *Home* from going into a death roll.

"Keep trimming!" Dad shouts.

"For what direction? Where is it coming from?"

"I don't know. Everywhere. Just keep trimming."

And that is where we're at when life, BEC (Before Everything Changed) lets go and tips into life, AEC (After Everything Changed).

All the falling apart of what used to be real? All the erupting of new facts of existence that never before existed on Earth? It all starts now.

THE TIPPING

TURNS OUT, THESE STORM CLOUDS are not your usual squall event. Turns out, they are an as yet unnamed weather system never before known to meteorology. And it has the power to open like a jaw of broken teeth, spit needles of frigid rain into your scalp, and thrash your sail like the tail of a pissed-off dragon.

"Kally! Let go!" Dad yells.

I let go the mainsheet, but it's too late to spill the air bomb. It presses *Home*'s sail over and down onto the sea. We're in a death roll. Our mast isn't pointing up anymore. It's pointing sideways and smashing into angry, heaving waves.

Our bodies pitch dizzily toward the foam. Dad grabs me by my sweatshirt, only to lose his grip when *Home* fails to stop at capsizing. She keeps rolling until she turtles. As in, her mast is buried in the water, pointing to the bottom of the sea.

When I force my eyes to open, I'm looking through eight feet of churning ocean at *Home*'s upside-down deck. It's rocking violently above my head. I see no sign of Dad.

I scissor kick against the downward pull of the entire Gulf of Maine, and by the time my fingers touch the planks of the deck, my lungs are fire. The impulse to inhale is excruciating, but I walk my hands methodically along the deck, aiming for the murky glow of daylight beyond *Home*'s railing. Just like Dad taught me.

Inches from my face, Dad's fist plunges into the water and closes around the shoulder strap of my life jacket. With a sharp yank, he pulls me into air and light and shoves me up onto the hull.

One hand locked onto my life jacket and the other around *Home*'s keel. I gasp air between the blasts of salt spray and try to clear my stinging eyes. Dad hacks up sea water. Our foreheads are touching. I'm so glad he's right there, I actually smile.

Choking and coughing, Dad nods toward the island. I squint through the hailstones that are bouncing off the hull in time to see Stuart execute a flying run down the steps that connect the clifftop to the beach. He bounds across the sand and sprints the length of the pier. Despite my very messed up circumstances, I can't help appreciating the streak of fluid movement he becomes as he vaults into the ocean rowboat, frees its tether, and digs its oars into the chop.

I'm going to meet the small blob that I watched in the binoculars. He's rowing powerfully in our direction.

First, I stumble on hailstones. Then, I trip on the dragging tail of the blanket that Stuart's mom wound around me when his dad pulled us out of the rowboat and up onto the pier. We're crossing the soggy grounds of East Ledge Lighthouse, headed for the shelter of the keeper's house.

The salt water from my wet clothes has soaked the blanket and I shiver past the peeling stucco walls of the lighthouse. As we come up on the tight group of small service buildings, Ollie runs ahead, excited about everything.

"And look, there's a satellite dish on the roof of that old radio shack," she calls over her shoulder. "That's because no phones can work here. And there's that big picnic table over there and, oh yeah, here's the best ever—we've got a whole weather station! With remote sensing devices!" She runs to the lawn fronting the radio shack. "See all these NOAA instruments over here on these poles? This one is for—"

"Ollie! We need to take Kally and David inside so they can dry off," Jennifer says with her mom voice.

"This place is so cool," Ollie bubbles as she snaps photos of the backside of the squall line that shipwrecked us. It is greyish green and ragged. But behind it, the skies in the east are cloudless and late August brilliant.

And, it's freezing.

I clutch the dripping blanket tighter over my dripping clothes. Dad reaches to blot my wet hair with his blanket, but I pull away. It's too soaked to dry anything. Besides, it's embarrassing.

"Are you sure that you're OK?" he asks.

"I'm fine." But it's true only in the loosest sense. I reach up and tug purple seaweed out of my hair as we pass by the radio shack.

That's when I hear it for the first time. Although "hearing" is not exactly right. I'm not sure it's even a sound. It's more of a—sound-feeling. A deep rumbling starts at my feet, rises through my chest, and ends with a fluttering vibration in my ears.

I slow down and look around. No one else seems to be feeling it. When I pass the radio shack, I look east, out beyond the cliff for some sign of what could be making the peculiar sensation. But all there is to see is *Home*—capsized and lurching in the heaving seas. The tears start instantly. They blur my view of our boat. And when they stuff my nose and ears, I lose track of the sound-feeling.

I stumble, this time over vacation gear that is scattered along the sandy path to the main house. I try hard to re-focus on what's at my feet. But images swirl in my mind: Stuart, spotting Dad and me from this very spot, where he had a clear view—both spectacular and embarrassing—of two near-drowned sailors clinging to their turtled boat; Stuart, dropping the bags of gear I just tripped on; Stuart, springing into superhero mode, bounding down the—

Stuart swoops beneath my blanket-wrapped arms, lifts away the tote bag I'm about to step on and swings it over to Ollie. "Bring this inside, Ollie. You can take pictures later."

I realize this is the first time I have heard Stuart's voice. He didn't speak a word during the entire rescue mission. It's a clear voice, all business.

Ollie refuses to look away from her camera. "I need

pictures of those atypical clouds for my report."

"Later. Here." Stuart drops the tote bag at her side.

"Stuart? You've been in a hurry since before we left home," Jennifer scolds. "Let's just slow down now. So much has happened."

"He can't wait to get our vacation over so he can go where he really wants to be," Ollie says, and keeps taking photos.

Stuart pushes the bag of beach towels into his sister's arms, then grasps multiple duffels in each hand and strides into the house. The rest of us file through the door behind him.

Stuart's mother was right. I haven't seen him stand still for a second, either though the binoculars or now in his presence. Liquid motion runs through this guy's veins. At the moment, he is a graceful blur doing a walk-through of the keeper's house. I guess he didn't have time to check it out before Dad and I shipwrecked on his doorstep.

Inside, the cedar shingled main house is spare and clean. Functional is the word. It has a large square kitchen equipped with dining table, cabinets with no doors, propane gas burner and fridge. A compact hand pump sits on the edge of the sink for bringing water up from the well.

Off the kitchen, there's a sitting room with wood stove, shelves of books, sofa, rocker, and a ladder that serves as stairs to the second floor.

Ollie runs into the sitting room and up the ladder. Her footsteps skitter overhead.

Jennifer hurries to the pump and fills the tea kettle with

water. "Your lips were so blue," she says.

"It's much better now, Mrs., um, Ms...."

"Hart. But please, it's Jennifer, and Mark. Let's get you into dry clothes."

In the thirty seconds we have been indoors, Stuart disappeared from the kitchen and came back dressed in dry sweats and T-shirt. Their large and colorful NASA logos are hard to miss. He pulls a second T-shirt and pair of pants from his backpack and pivots in my direction—only to bump into his mom, who is holding out a set of her own clothes.

I don't realize that I have erupted into awkward laughter until it is too late. I never laugh that way. Maybe I did it now because my dad and I are dripping salt water puddles across the Harts' kitchen floor and otherwise crashing their family vacation. Or maybe it's because ever since Stuart landed us at the pier, Jennifer has had this look on her face—the one that says she never imagined strangers would strand themselves on the private lighthouse island she just spent a large chunk of her family's income to rent.

I suppress my involuntary behavior and cringe to think how long I've been standing here, eyes shuttling between the neatly folded suburban summer outfit on offer from Jennifer, and the NASA branded T-shirt and jeans hanging from Stuart's index finger.

Jennifer reads the part of my mind that has not gone blank. "I won't take it personally," she says, with a warm smile. "Your choice."

When I reach for Stuart's clothes, we make eye contact—which is intense—until he realizes that's what we're doing and turns away. "Thank you," I say to the side of his head. I pivot to Jennifer and say, "Thank you both."

Mark comes into the kitchen carrying a dry sweatshirt and pants for my dad. "These should fit, more or less."

"Thanks," Dad says, taking them.

"Now get out of those wet clothes," Jennifer says. She transfers food from the coolers to the fridge. "I'll heat water for hot drinks. After you've warmed up, we can talk about how to get you home."

Stuart strides to the odd, built-in nook of space that occupies the far corner of the kitchen. It holds a bunk bed and a small porthole window facing the sea. He pitches his backpack up onto the mattress and springs in next to it. Then, he slides open the window curtain and wipes the glass clean with his hand. Finally, he comes to a full stop.

Ollie runs out of the sitting room, scurries across the kitchen, and climbs the ladder to the bunk. "I want to sleep here." She squeezes into the nook next to Stuart.

Jennifer looks up from pumping water into the kettle. "Stuart is sleeping there, Ollie."

The bathroom seems to be the only choice for where to change clothes. But that means I must walk across the entire kitchen while pretending there is nothing odd about carrying Stuart's clothing in there with me.

"Why does *he* get the best place to sleep? Just because he's leaving?" Ollie pouts.

For some reason, as I slink toward the bathroom door, I feel curious about where it is that Stuart is going. When I reach for the latch, I look over my shoulder and catch Mark and Jennifer exchanging that parental look—the one that says, "we have to talk." Lately, my own parents have been flinging that same look between them.

I glance across the room at Stuart. He missed the whole thing. He is tucked inside the bunk, focused on his phone and ignoring the way he is being discussed as if he's not here. Suddenly, I feel an urge to warn him about whatever it is that he doesn't see coming.

"Stuart gets to sleep up there because he won't fall out," Mark says.

"Now come down and let your brother get settled," Jennifer adds firmly.

I back my way into the bathroom and close the wood panel door—which is so thin, I might as well still be in the kitchen.

"The WiFi here looks good. I'll call the keeper," I hear Stuart announce.

Mark's voice: "We're supposed to use the satellite dish to make calls. Like Ollie said, there's no cell service this far out."

"The weather forecast was for perfect weather this week," Dad says. He sounds stunned and like he's registering only half of what is going on.

I hear Ollie's sneakers meet the floor and scamper across the kitchen as she says, "I never saw clouds look like those. I told the keeper that when I was taking their pictures. He said, 'lots of things these days I've never seen before.' Then he said he normally shows people around 'but the sea is changing.' And then he left. And then, the temperature dropped twenty degrees in three minutes. Hey, I bet those instruments out there recorded the whole thing."

The screen door swings and bangs.

Jennifer's voice: "Our Ollie has a weather obsession. She's been this way since she was five."

Mark's voice: "The keeper isn't answering?"

Stuart's voice: "It says his number is not available."

Mark sounds like he's reading: "Composting toilet, propane fridge, kerosene hurricane lamps. In case of emergency—here, Stuart, here's the keeper's email. Try that."

Jennifer: "Who wants tea and who wants coffee?"

I stop listening. My full concentration is required to decipher what I'm seeing in the mirror. Salt-crusted hair with a ribbon of seaweed. Shoulders caved forward under a heavy wet blanket into a posture Mom would yell at me for. Bruised and scratched hands holding the jeans and T-shirt of a stranger—who is strangely interesting.

I strip off my sagging T-shirt and sailing pants, rinse salt from my face and hands, and pull Stuart's size L items of official NASA outerwear over my damp, size M underwear. I'm thankful that it seems he thought twice before loaning his intimates to me.

My mind is both dazed and racing, a state I didn't know it could have. It replays the last hour in slo-mo, fast-forward, and even backwards while my arms pull up Stuart's jeans. I feel like I'm still under water when I bend over to turn up the cuffs. Way up.

I become aware of the voices outside my door again. If I hadn't just lived through the events they're talking about, I'd think they were describing some other world.

"So then, after the big wave…," I hear Jennifer say.

Dad: "I thought we could put in here and rest up for a couple hours."

Mark: "We were nearly here when you say the wave passed you. We didn't run into anything like that."

Dad: "It was moving northeast to southwest. You would have been coming up on East Ledge from the south. The island deflected the wave. By the time you rounded the tip, it was miles away. Kally and I reset our course for the pier, but the wind died, and we were struggling against a current that was not on any of our charts. A few minutes later, gusts came from every direction at once."

I hear Ollie call in through the screen door with the obvious question. "How can the wind even do that?"

Dad's version of an answer is: "I've been sailing since I was your age. I never saw wind act that way."

Finished with rolling my cuffs, make that, Stuart's cuffs, I face the mirror again. I'm drowning in Stuart's T-shirt. As I turn up its short sleeves, I examine the logo emblazoned across my chest: NASA Institute for Space Studies. My sailing pants are in a puddle on the floor, and when I bend over to gather them up, I flinch at the sickening sound of my phone ricocheting off of the claw-foot bathtub.

Mark is asking Dad, "Are you and Kally on vacation, too?"

"Just the weekend. We slept on the boat last night."

I lift my phone off the floor, steel myself, and press the power button. It oozes water. The home screen photo of Mom flickers. It's the one of her brushing her hair away from her eyes, movie star style, so that she can show off the bracelet I made for her birthday last month.

I notice that the beads are the same blue as the reflections in her eyes. I suspect that, without realizing it, that's why I chose them. More than anything right now, I want to be with her and my dad. In our own house. I squeeze my eyes closed to fend off a new round of tears.

When my mind finally gets a grip, it declares: *time to go home.*

But, as I close my hand around the door latch, the screen on my phone flashes. Mom's photo strobes, then pixelates. On the other side of the bathroom door, Dad is saying, "Our plan was to head home about now. Kally's new school is taking the seniors on college tours next week."

I stare at the fractured photo of Mom and wait to hear my dad say what he should say next—what he *would* say if everything was OK with my family and those "something is wrong" vibes that I've been getting were false alarms. I wait to hear my father tell the Harts the biggest reason we need to leave their island as soon as possible.

But he doesn't.

Whatever he wasn't telling me this morning, it must be about him and my mother. I stuff the thought and fumble with the door latch. Bursting into the kitchen, I look straight at Dad and announce: "But *really*, we have got to head home right now. So we can be at the airport tomorrow morning to pick up Mom."

Stuart looks up from the email he was writing to the keeper because, like everyone else in this suddenly very crowded kitchen, he finds it hard to ignore the semi-hysterical person.

Everyone else, that is, except for Dad. He brushes past me on his way into the bathroom while avoiding my eyes for the second time this morning. The door closes behind him.

When I turn back to the kitchen, I look from Mark to Jennifer, then lock eyes with Stuart. I can tell he is gauging the tension between me and my dad. He is also trying *not* to check me out as I stand here dressed in his clothes.

Jennifer makes a brave attempt to ease the situation. "You must have been so scared out there," she ventures in a high voice, clears her throat, and hands me a cup of tea.

I wrap my hands around the warmth of the cup like it's a lifeline.

From inside the bathroom, Dad announces to the world, "Kally knew that rogue wave was coming before we saw it."

I grip the cup harder and glare at the bathroom door. I *did not* know the wave was coming. Saying so makes me sound like something I'm not. I continue to glare at the door as I weigh options for how to deal with a dad who no longer seems capable of being real with me. I wish that overdue conversation could have happened, the one the wave put an end to just as Dad finally started to talk.

I keep on glaring, because I'm dumbfounded at how everyone in this kitchen is dancing around the topic of how fully weird this morning is—except for Ollie. Am I the only one who's bothered by the way nothing and nobody is behaving like they should? Not the ocean, or the weather, or Stuart's parents, or my dad—or *me*?

Gradually, I pick up on the mortifying fact that Stuart has been watching me this whole time. Who does he see me to be as I stand here, not acting like myself? Maybe we are all failing to be real with each other because, deep inside, we're in the same state that *Home* is in—totally unmoored, adrift in whatever it is that's—

"How did you do that?" Stuart asks. His question halts my binge of self-absorption. "How did you know the wave was coming?"

I have no way to answer, because *it's not like that*. I pretend I didn't hear him and proceed to towel my hair with my wet clothes.

"Let her catch her breath, Stuart," Jennifer says. "You must be starved, Kally. The sandwiches are almost ready."

"Thank you." I stop rubbing my pants on my head.

Dad steps out of the bathroom carrying his soggy, balled up sailing shorts and shirt and looking fully ridiculous dressed in Mark's polo shirt and golf pants.

Stuart's phone beeps. "It's the keeper," he says.

I whirl to face Stuart. "Is he on his way? Should we go down to the pier?"

Stuart reads his phone screen. "He says his boat hit a breakwater in the storm. It will take him a few days to fix the propeller shaft. He could hire a guy to come out and get you this afternoon, but that would cost you a lot. Or, you can wait until he fixes his boat. He guesses he could pick you up in three or four days."

While "three or four days" reverberates in my head without quite registering, I hear Mark ask, "That's it?"

"He ends with: 'you folks have a real good week,'" Stuart says.

"I'm sorry," Dad says, looking at Jennifer, then Mark, but not at me. "I know this is your vacation, but if it's OK with you, Kally and I could camp down on the beach—"

"Dad," I croak, and shoot him the most searing "what is wrong with you" look ever.

Finally, he brings himself to look at me. "I could at least try to salvage *Home*, Kally. There's no replacing her—you know that."

Jennifer and Mark wear the expressions of two overworked parents in the midst of realizing that their break from it all has just flipped into the total opposite. Mark opens the refrigerator and pulls out two cans of beer. "You're welcome to stay, of course." He hands one can to Dad, pops open the other, and takes a long drink.

"Of course," Jennifer nods as she sets out cheese, lettuce, and tomato sandwiches. "Um, I think we could make that work," she says slowly. "Between what we brought, and the things other people left in the cupboards, I guess there would be enough food—"

"No. We can't stay," I snap. I grab Dad's clothes out of his hands and bunch them together with mine. "My mom is coming home tomorrow morning. We are going to the airport. We are going to pick her up." I'm being loud and emphatic, as if that will make it real—make it stick.

The Harts must wonder why I am growing more unhinged each second. But Dad knows why. And finally, he acts like it.

"Kally, let's take a walk," he says, as if I'm someone he is trying to talk off a ledge.

Dad swings the screen door open, and as I make my graceless exit, he tells the Harts, "We appreciate everything you have done for us. And Stuart, I can't thank you enough. Excuse us, Kally and I need to talk."

BROKEN

 of North America in the Gulf of Maine on an island that is as good as empty, and I have never been more desperate to get space.

I walk as fast as I can across the grounds, the wet wad of Dad's and my clothes clutched against my chest. They quickly turn Stuart's NASA sweats and T-shirt damp and sea weedy.

"We should hang those in the sun," Dad says, striding to keep up with me.

I storm past the quaint clothesline and on toward the far end of the grounds where the lighthouse hugs the edge of the bluff.

"If my phone wasn't drowned, I would call the keeper right now. I would tell him to find that guy who's got the only working boat left back there and I would hire him myself," I call over my shoulder. "We have got to get back.

We have got to pick up Mom."

I reach the base of the lighthouse tower. If I go much further, I'll pitch over the sandy point of the cliff. I pace circles instead. My arms ache from pressing the wet clothes tighter to my chest with each step.

On one of my revolutions, I spot Stuart standing in the doorway of the keeper's house, watching Dad watching me. And why shouldn't Stuart do that? We're a one ring circus. Still, I wish he would go inside.

My tantrum does some good because at last Dad gets it that—yeah—it's time for some truth-telling. "Kally, listen," he says, "we don't have to rush to get back. Your mom isn't coming home tomorrow."

So, there it is. This is what the drawings in my sketchbook were trying to tell me. This—Dad's news flash—is what they knew was coming. My drawings aren't broken after all. In fact, their tangled twistedness is the spitting image of how this moment feels. While that might prove I am not crazy, it does little to quiet my rising panic.

I spin to face Dad head on. "What do you mean Mom is not coming home tomorrow? She said she was. She'll be waiting for us at the airport and we'll be stuck out here—"

"Your mother is mad at me."

"She's mad at you," I repeat flatly. I'm trying to take in the fact that, apparently, Dad's secret has a Part Two. "Great. What did you do?" I intone, like I'm the lawyer and he's the accused.

"I disappointed her." From the sound of it, any emotion he had about that wore itself out a while ago. He looks across the water and his eyes catch on *Home*. She's grounded on a sandbar. Abandoned. "This isn't how I planned to talk with you—"

"Wait. You needed a plan?"

My mind races to prepare for what must be coming next—Dad's secret, Part Three. What did he do to make her so mad and disappointed that she won't come home? Why does he need a plan for telling me whatever he has been keeping from me?

I think the worst. Then, I remember my friend's stories about the things *their* parents needed plans for telling them—and I think the very worst.

"Am I going to be mad at you, too?" I demand, my face twisting in disgust. "Is that why you are so afraid to say—"

"What?" Dad looks genuinely confused. Then, his eyes get wide. "Oh, no. No. Nothing like that, Kally."

It's a convincing denial. I clench our soggy clothes tighter still against my body. "So, what then? What is Part Three of the Guthrie family secret? You two are breaking up?"

"Of course not! No, Kally, your mom needs time, that's all."

Needing time is never the whole story, my mind screams, while my wavering voice says, "That's what everybody says when—"

"But we're not, Kally."

Suddenly, I'm crushingly sad. "Why didn't she tell *me* she was mad at you? Before she went to install her show—she could have—"

"But she couldn't. She had already left. It happened over the phone."

My patience snaps. Why are we playing twenty questions? Why have I let myself dance around the mysterious *something* that I felt coming? The *something* that's been on its way for days. The *something* creeping into my sketchbook and freaking out my drawings, making it impossible for me to picture myself leaving my parents and going to college next year. The *something* that could be the beginning of the end of my family—

"*What* happened over the phone?" I demand.

"Your mom and I have started to see a few things differently."

He *can't* believe that's an answer.

"Everybody says that," I'm shouting now. "When, really, they are—"

"But I told you, we're *not*," he says, raising his voice.

Over Dad's shoulder, I see Stuart carrying pillows and blankets from the keeper's house to the radio shack. He's being polite enough not to stare at the strangers melting down next to his lighthouse. But I'm sure he can hear everything. We must be the Hart family's worst nightmare. I bet they wish they were setting up their badminton net. Instead they've had to feed their meager food supplies to two dysfunctional wash-ashores who oozed sea water across their kitchen floor before going outside to off-load moldy family baggage in voices loud enough to wake the mainland—

My latest binge of self-absorption is—yeah—disgustingly self-absorbed. To distract myself from myself, I set to untangling the wad of clothes that I'm still clutching. Then, I straighten my back and rearrange my face to as near normal as possible, just in case Stuart looks over here again.

"OK, I get it. We do not need to be at the airport in the morning. Mom is not coming back tomorrow. She is mad at you. You do not see something the way she does. So, when *is* she coming back?"

"She wouldn't say."

I stop fidgeting with the clothes and stare at him. What sort of emergency management is this? I search his face and I plead, "What are you doing to fix it?" But what I see in his eyes is that he has no plan for fixing it. "Really?" I squint even harder at him and his silence. And suddenly I know, there's more.

A sickening knot twists through my stomach. I want him to tell me what it is—right now. I wait. But his eyes have gone blank. He's got no words for whatever the *more* is.

I wipe the tears from my cheeks with our clammy clothes and push them into Dad's hands. I storm to the cliff's edge and, splattering squish from my sneakers, stomp every wooden step down to the beach.

One hundred yards offshore, *Home* rocks on her side against the sandbar. She is clinging, still, to the lower half of her mast. But the top half is nowhere to be seen. There's no telling where else she is broken.

Even so, I'm glad to see her. She's wrecked, but she is one of the few things from my life, BEC, that I can still recognize. I plant myself in the damp sand at water's edge and start my vigil on *Home*, searching for any sign that, when Dad said we could salvage her, it was not just wishful thinking.

The sky overhead is a shade of green that does not belong up there. Down on the horizon, a thick slash of clouds the color of purple charcoal is tearing its way north.

I try to identify what class of clouds they are. I'm sure that I've seen them before. A few more seconds of scrutiny and I realize that I *have* seen them before. They look like the ghoulish scratchings I've been making in my sketchbook the last couple of weeks. If the sky could have scars, they would be these clouds

Now, I'm keeping vigil on our boat *and* the scar clouds.

I shade my eyes and squint at *Home* through the sun sparkles that span the water between us. I wish I could stop replaying that highly unreal conversation I just had with Dad. Nothing about it was like him. Or my mom. Or me.

My stomach flip-flops. I stand and kick at the sand. The signals haven't stopped pouring in. There's something *more*—something *else*—coming. This gnawing feeling isn't only about my family.

My sketchbook is out there on *Home*. I need it here with me. Maybe, if I tried again to draw what I'm—

I sense motion on my right. A figure is jogging toward me up the beach. I stiffen. But it's only Stuart.

I take a few deep breaths and resume the watch. Tides go out fast here. I can see more of *Home*'s broken body every minute.

Stuart runs up alongside me, downshifts, and paces in the sand, catching his breath. "I moved my stuff into to the shack. You can have the bunk in the kitchen." He's breathing hard and wiping sweat off his face with the neck of his T-shirt.

"In other words, we're staying."

"A few days. Until the keeper can come for you. I overheard your dad."

I nod.

What existed solely in the realm of the unreal a few hours ago is growing more real by the second. Real enough to impose its own twisted logic: Mom is not coming home tomorrow. Therefore, no rush to get home. I am not due at school until next week to get on that bus with the other seniors and tour colleges in the name of my life's Big Dream—which, unlike everyone else, I've been mortifyingly unable to imagine for myself. Therefore, Dad and I might as well stay right here and attempt to salvage our boat. Which got wrecked by a weather event from another planet—this one. Therefore, I am talking to a complete stranger named Stuart Hart while wearing his astronaut outfit.

"You've got to be beyond hungry." Stuart pulls a power bar from his pocket and offers it to me.

I am. I reach for it and say, "Thanks. And, thanks for the dry clothes."

"Sure.

"And—yeah—for saving our lives."

Stuart takes a long look at *Home* and sits down on the sand. I tear open the wrapper and figure that as long as I'm on the subject of Dad and me being here, it's a good time to apologize. Through bites of solidified peanut butter, I say, "Sorry we're messing up your vacation."

"No worries there. My expectations for this one were not all that high."

I'm about to ask why not, but, like I said, we're barely more than strangers.

I take another bite of the bar as my eyes travel from the NASA logo that runs the length of Stuart's pants leg, to the one on the front of his hat, to the third one on the T-shirt

I'm wearing, and—yeah—to the fourth one on the power bar wrapper in my hand.

"That vacation to NASA sure was a hit," I say.

He smiles. I note: *first time I have seen Stuart smile.* Then I ask myself, why am I keeping count of things Stuart does?

"It wasn't a vacation," he says. "It was a tour of the Space Center. I'm doing my senior year at NASA. Right after this lighthouse family vacation, I head to Houston to start the internship."

"You want to be an astronaut?"

"Flight Controller. For the 2045 human-piloted Mars mission."

He says it like that is the easiest thing ever. I don't mean the part about going to Mars—I mean the part about knowing precisely what he wants to do with his life.

"You?" he asks as if, like him, I have a closetful of clothes plastered with logos declaring the nature of my life's purpose and deepest aspirations and the only reason I'm not dressed in my logo wear is because it's temporarily marooned on a sandbar.

"I mean, what are you into, besides sailing?" he says, trying again. But not in a pushy way. I'm beginning to think he is genuinely interested in what I'm into. "Like, how did you know that rogue wave was coming?" he adds.

So, *that's* what he's curious about. My eyes narrow as I look over at Stuart to see if his question is real or if he's entertaining himself.

"Your dad said you knew it was there before you saw it. How did you do that?"

There's something in how Stuart is talking to me—the tone in his voice, the energy coming from him—it feels real.

He isn't making fun of me. He thinks I really *did* know the rogue wave was coming. Maybe, I did.

I look at the waves breaking on *Home* and along the sandbar, pry off my soggy shoes, dig my toes deep into the sand, and take a stab at explaining the unexplainable.

"Honestly, I didn't know what was coming. But I knew that *something* was. That happens to me a lot." I gauge whether that qualified as too much information. But the straightforward energy coming from Stuart holds steady. If anything, it just got more supportive. I would hate to scare it away. So, I quickly add, "It's not like I have visions." I try not to sound defensive. "I don't see the future. It's nothing like that. It's just, I make these drawings. My mom says they're abstractions. But they're not. They're actual things. Only, they're *flickering* things—things changing directions, mixing with what is around them, turning into something else. I mean, I draw things that aren't what they used to be anymore, but they aren't what they're going to be either…yet." My voice trails off.

That sounded weird, even to me. If *that* doesn't scare him away, it must be because he's the kind of guy who actually looks forward to going to Mars. I simulate a bit of casual laughter but end up coughing.

Stuart isn't laughing, and he doesn't seem scared. He seems to be deep in thought, like he's trying to solve a math problem. As I watch him thinking, something happening on the sandbar behind him catches my attention and snaps me back to here and now.

I scramble to my feet, spraying sand and water all over Stuart, and bound into the surf.

"Where are you going?" Stuart calls after me.

"The tide is finally out," I shout over my shoulder.

"Yeah? So? Hey! My dry clothes!"

But I'm already waist-deep and pushing my way toward *Home.* I look back and see Stuart hesitate, then plunge in.

By the time our feet touch the steep slope of the sandbar, the water is up to my chest and I'm half wading, half swimming. I climb up onto the bar, then dash across the wet, packed sand to where *Home* lurches in the rough surf. I wade out to her, lock onto her rail, haul myself out of the swirling surf, and flop into the swamped cockpit.

Bracing myself against the pitching deck, I work to free the anchor from the deck locker. As I'm straining to lift the anchor over the rail, Stuart appears beside me. He grabs one end and, together, we heave the dead weight out onto the sandbar.

I crab-walk toward the cabin door and drag it open against the weight of water sloshing in *Home*'s cockpit. When it's ajar just enough, I grab my bag of gear and swing it behind me to Stuart. I reach back in to retrieve Dad's gear bag, but a rolling wave knocks *Home* into a wild lurch, sending us both crash landing onto the deck. Stuart jumps back up, steadies himself, and aims for the cabin door. I grab his arm.

"Let's go," I shout over the surf.

"We can save more of your stuff," he says, pulling Dad's bag from the cabin. "There's more in here that I can—"

"No! The tide has started coming again, fast." I make eye contact with him and shout each word: "There are rogue waves out here."

Half carrying, half floating the bags we salvaged, we allow the gentler surges on this side of the sandbar to push us toward shore. Stuart keeps turning around to eye the breakers that pound against *Home*. It's the first time I've seen him look unsteady.

He might be an astronaut, but he's not a sailor.

ST. ELMO'S VISIT

FINALLY, THE DAY EVERYTHING CHANGED burns itself into a smoldering heap of dusk. This is the hottest it's been, despite the fact that sunset happened half an hour ago. Which I missed. I was busy washing sand and crusty salt out of the formerly clean and dry NASA clothing that Stuart entrusted to me this morning.

Thanks to the gear bags we recovered from *Home* this afternoon, I'm wearing my own clothes. That alone is worth the exhausting trip to the sandbar. The sweats and shirt that I just draped over the clothesline are dripping due to the lack of spin dry here on East Ledge Island. But this heat will parch them fast enough, even without the sun. I tried to convince Stuart to let me wash the clothes he sacrificed during our salvage mission. After all, I'm the one who decided to wade out to *Home*. But his face flooded with embarrassment at, I guess, the thought of me doing his laundry with my bare hands. It was endearing. Anyway, he did his own, then disappeared inside the radio shack to finish setting up his new sleeping quarters.

Dad has spread the contents of his recovered gear bag across the double-wide picnic table to dry. I haven't gone over to help. I'm trying to decide how angry I should be at him for treating me like I am ten years old and not telling me what's going on with him and Mom. Also, I suspect he's concentrating on more than the contents of the bag. I hope he is. I hope he's devising an emergency plan for how to fix things with Mom. I'm not going to risk interrupting that, even though I have a hundred questions. He's working by the yellow light that spills from the windows of the keeper's house. When the lighthouse beam sweeps past, it bathes him in a soft glow that reflects off puffy low clouds.

If I snapped a photo of the scene, it could pass for a sentimental postcard of a tranquil summer night on a romantically deserted island. But only because postcards are silent. That sound-feeling is back, and I would not call it tranquil or romantic.

Trying to zero in on it, I turn my ears toward the sea, then back to the island. But the only sound I locate is the creak of Mark's rocking chair in the sitting room. I can hear everything else going on in there too, not because I'm trying to—but because the air and the sea have fallen dead still in the heat. And now, so does the sound-feeling.

"I know it's hot in here, but I love these things," Jennifer says. I hear a match strike, and the kerosene lamp sputter. I glance over at the window. Mark is in the rocker, reading a thick technical book. "I thought you couldn't wait to read a novel this week." Jennifer stacks sheets and pillows on the sofa, so my dad can sleep there, I guess.

"We have to talk to Stuart," Mark says, and keeps on reading.

Jennifer lowers her voice, "If we tell them we need to talk—you know, as a family—I'm sure they'll give us some space."

They must be my dad and me. Who else could it be? This is so awkward. Stuart's mom carries the kerosene lamp past the window and into the kitchen.

In the quiet that follows, I take a deep breath and get as motionless as I can, hoping to catch the sound-feeling again. But all I hear is Ollie thumping her way down the ladder to the sitting room.

"I made my bed," Ollie announces. "There's a window right next to it. I hung my thermometer out of it. The temperature went up 37 degrees Fahrenheit since we got here." She sounds excited to her core.

The ancient AM radio squawks static from the sitting room bookshelf, then settles on a scratchy station. A rousing sailors' work song fades in and out through the tinny speaker, and I give up on trying to solve the mystery of the sound-feeling. Instead, I wring more water out of the clothes I've hung on the line.

"Show me your room," Jennifer says to Ollie, and I hear them head up the ladder to the second floor.

Over at the picnic table, Dad has gotten even more engrossed in gear sorting. It's his body's tried-and-true way of chilling out. In spite of how seriously messed up things are, I decide it's time for me to chill, too.

I haul my rescued dry bag into the main house and fill my water bottle at the sink pump. Then, I climb the four steps of the ladder to the odd little kitchen bunk that Stuart gallantly sacrificed for my sake. It's a tight squeeze and the wood paneling grazes the top of my head. But I can see how it would be a comfy place to sleep—if only its dead air space wasn't harboring a summer's worth of musty heat.

I hunch over my sea bag and locate my sketchbook. It's damp from its encounter with this morning's rogue wave—which feels like weeks ago. But the waterproofing did a heroic job of saving it from further ruin. Cheered by the sight of it, I try not to rip its soggy cover as I coax pages to open.

Dad comes into the house carrying his emptied gear bag. At the sink, he fills a glass with water and chugs it. "The humidity must be in single digits. It's the desert out there," he says, to me, I guess.

I don't look up. I would prefer not to acknowledge the unnatural lack of humidity in the North Atlantic right now—much less all the other things that seem to be going haywire. And, I'm crashing tired. Not to mention, the pages of my sketchbook are stuck together, and I have to peel them apart one by one.

"Think we can make it back out to *Home* tomorrow?" Dad asks. "At low tide?"

I guess I should say something.

"Yeah."

"We'll assess her damages." He's trying to sound as upbeat about that as possible.

"Yeah."

"OK. I'll go and finish up. My gear is dry enough to repack." He waits for a second in case I'm going to say something, but I'm not.

The fat spring attached to the screen door twangs as he leaves. I chug well water from my water bottle. It tastes like iron.

The spring on the door twangs again and Stuart comes in. He bee-lines to the sink pump, fills his water bottle and holds it to his neck. He pivots, then strides back across the kitchen toward the door. On his way past my bunk, I catch him stealing a look at my sketchbook where I laid it open on the blanket to dry. He's raised his eyebrow as if he's surprised—and maybe even impressed—by what he sees.

I look down at the water-wrinkled page of furiously drawn lines.

Stuart continues on to the window beside the screen door and opens it wide. "You know those drawings you said you've been making? The ones your mom thinks are abstractions, but you say are actual things?"

"They *are* actual things. They're actual things in the middle of *changing*."

"Yeah, right." He finds a stick on the sill and props open the window. "That's why I've been thinking that—what you've got there are diagrams of force fields," he says as if, of course, anyone would think that.

Some science class at one point or other left traces in my memory about force fields, and I try to retrieve them.

"I, I uh, I can't see how, I wouldn't know—"

I hate that I'm stammering, but Stuart has come over to the bunk, and now he's standing at my shoulder, looking right at my sketchbook—the most personal and private object in my entire life.

I close the book and glare at him.

"Sorry. Small house," he says. The way Stuart steps back

to give me and my sketchbook space makes me think he truly *is* sorry.

He retreats to the open window and leans out just as Ollie skips into the kitchen, then wriggles into the window frame beside her brother.

"Hey, look at that," Stuart says to Ollie. He points out the window at the sky.

I peer through the small porthole above my bunk. There's lightning in the distance. Lots of it.

"What's the forecast?" Stuart asks Ollie.

"Hot, clear and dry—according to that old radio in the other room," Ollie chirps.

"Grab your logbook. Let's go see what it is according to you."

Thrilled at Stuart's invitation, Ollie disappears into the sitting room and comes back toting a large black book. It looks seriously official.

From my bunk, I watch through the screen door as Stuart and Ollie make their way past Dad and the picnic table, across the sandy lawn, and over to the array of poles topped with weather instruments. Pulses of the lighthouse beam and distant, silent flashes of lightning illuminate the grounds erratically.

When I return to my sketchbook, the drawings in it look—different.

Force fields, he said.

I search my memory again. Now that Stuart isn't spying on my sketchbook, I start to remember fragments of what they told us in that science class. Magnetism, gravity, sound, electricity. Those things are waves. When they spread out through space, they make fields of waves. The fields can be huge like the wave fields of the ocean or gravity fields in space, or they can be beyond small like the field of electricity in a wire. Then, I remember why force fields are such a big deal. The energy of their moving waves *changes* things that get caught in them—even across great distances.

All of that is why crackling music is coming from the sitting room. Radio waves are moving through space from a station that could be anywhere. They're hitting the little antenna and getting turned into electrical waves inside the radio. Those electrical waves make the radio's speaker vibrate, and that makes sound waves move through the air and into the kitchen. They hit my eardrums. My brain turns them into electrical brain waves. And my mind registers them as annoying sea chanties.

I would not want to take a test on it, but that's what I remember about force fields. It's a bit of a drag to learn that, when Stuart stole a look at my drawing, it reminded him of a science fair project. Instead of, I don't know, something more *artful*, I guess.

I'm trying to feel better about that when the sound-feeling creeps into my awareness again. This time, maybe because it's dark, it gives me a sensation of sweeping vastness. I swivel my head like it's a radar dish. My bunk-cave must be acting as a huge ear, because I can tell that whatever the source of the sound-feeling might be, it is definitely coming from somewhere left of the sink. And that means…northeast.

Exploding with curiosity, I stretch my senses to keep track of the sound as I climb down the ladder and inch across the kitchen to the screen door.

Outside, Stuart is holding a flashlight to the weather

instruments while Ollie writes notes in her log. "I didn't know birds flew around at night." Ollie says. She continues to write, nose buried in her logbook.

I stop at the threshold of the door and train my whole listening self on the sound-feeling. When the screeching breaks out overhead, it jolts me like an electrical shock. On its next sweep overhead, the lighthouse beam strobes off the white bellies of frenzied birds. Hundreds of them. Their delirious movements flash in and out of the light, making it impossible to tell what kind of birds they are. Veering and diving, they swarm out to sea. Straight toward the lightning. I push open the door to watch the creatures out-distance the circling beam and dissolve into the strobing blackness.

Ollie finally looks up from her note taking and says, "That's weird."

Like me, Stuart stands silently in the creepy wake of the birds' frenzy. Over at the picnic table, so does Dad. I'm not sure if that is because we're at a loss for words, or because we're getting used to weird.

The next time the lighthouse beam skims the sea, it lights up threads of white, rising vapors that have begun to dance offshore. It's as if dozens of smoldering campfires were floating and burning on the face of the ocean. A blaze of silent orange lightning slices the horizon.

Stuart hands off the flashlight to Ollie.

"Where are you going?" she asks.

He pulls his NASA cap out of his pocket and secures it on his head. "To get ready."

"For what?"

"Not sure."

Stuart looks over at the keeper's house and sees me at

the door.

"Ask Kally," he says, smiling, and heads for the radio shack.

Ollie starts in my direction, but a deep growl of suddenly close thunder pulls her up short. She reverses course and sprints to catch up with Stuart.

Those birds must be far out to sea by now. Wondering if this latest outbreak of strangeness has anything to do with the sound-feeling, I stretch my senses to search for it one more time. But all I pick up are the angry force fields of thunder surrounding us.

Finally finished repacking his gear bag, Dad comes over and stands beside me, fanning himself with his cap.

"I planned to give this to you this morning, on *Home.*" He places his cap on his head and holds a shiny new sketchbook up to the light from the sitting room windows. "It's for your college tours. I thought maybe you could use…you might need…"

He holds the book out to me with both hands and his eyes are right there, like they were this morning when we were clinging to *Home* and gulping air. I take the sketchbook and hug his neck.

Ollie comes out from the shack, her flashlight beam bobbing before her. Dad and I watch her train the light on the pole-top wind indicator. Its arrow sits motionless. She's about to turn away when the arrow jerks, then rotates a full 360 degrees.

A high-pitched zinging vibrates overhead. We see Ollie's flashlight beam sink until it points at the grass. She has become transfixed, eyes riveted on the roof. Dad and I step away from the house and look up.

Purple flames snap from the tip of the lightning rod. The smell of sulfur burns the inside of my nose.

In a husky whisper, Ollie intones: "St. Elmo's Fire." She shouts up to the second-floor windows of the house. "You guys!" She sprints past us and slams open the screen door.

Through the window, we can see her bound into the sitting room. She skids to a stop. She composes herself. And then she broadcasts from the bottom of the ladder to Jennifer and Mark's bedroom upstairs: "I have observed evidence of a strong electric field in the atmosphere!"

Dad turns from the window, smiling. He reaches for my hand and raises it above my head. Instantly, cold blue light sprouts from the tip of my finger. It jitters there, smaller than a candle flame. I think I hear it hissing. I hold my breath as tingles of electricity dance down my finger.

"Good omen for us sailors. Remember, Kally?" Dad asks.

I remember. Since I was ten, I have asked him to tell and retell that story, the one about glowing sparks of light that sometimes appear on ships' mastheads when lightning storms are near. And here's my finger, a miniature ship mast, channeling my own body's lightning-charged electrons up into the air.

I am beyond awestruck.

Ancient sailors called the phenomenon St. Erasmus, aka St. Elmo, patron saint of sailors, bringer of good luck. Tonight, I don't know what to make of that.

It's finally lights out in the main house, except for the dusty bulb that casts a glint of yellow on the walls of my bunk-cave. I sit on the thin mattress with the wall as a backrest. Each time my hair brushes the wood above my head, I'm sure it's spiders.

The thunder sounds no closer, but it has grown more constant. First, I was too worn out to sleep. Now, I'm too hot. The past seventeen hours have gridlocked my brain with thoughts and images of people, events, and straight up confusion. Plus, I can't stop replaying what Stuart said: he doesn't think my drawings are abstract art. He thinks they are force fields.

As the latest clap of thunder fades, I picture the years my family has lived life together as being one giant field of emotions and memories. Tonight, its waves are frothing and crashing over me. Wherever my mom is, my whole self is being affected by her force field, at a distance.

I look through my portal window and watch the lighthouse beam brush the ocean vapors. Somewhere in that vastness, something changed this morning. Something big. That untold event birthed a rogue wave, and it steamrolled into *Home*. Then, other rogue waves of temperatures, pressures, and wind directions converged at East Ledge Island. They spun themselves up into one mighty shipwrecking microburst. And that lightning out there right now? An electrical field, affecting our roof way over here, and making St. Elmo's fire fizz from my fingertip.

I look back at my sketchbook. Tonight, our planet is churning with forces that are off-balance. They're building into waves that could come to affect us from anywhere at any moment. That sound-feeling could be one of those forces.

I picture those things, but I don't draw any of them. My

new sketchbook from Dad lies on the pillow, open and looking up at me like a dare. I'm afraid to let my pen-holding hand go. I don't want to see, really see, the forces that Stuart says I am picking up. What if the frantic lines I have drawn since Mom left for the city are *her*, caught in the middle between what things were and what they are twisting and turning into? What if she needs help and she's trying to—

I slam the sketchbook shut. I don't want to sit in this airless bunk and draw. I don't want to be someone who feels force fields coming. I want Stuart to be 100% wrong. I want the lines he saw to be nothing more than my own snarled confusion about what's going on with my family, and— yeah—about this whole "life calling" thing and how I'm supposed to know what mine is.

But most of all, I want to talk to my parents. Not Dad. Not Mom. Both of them. As a team. *My* team.

I'm whining. How useless am I?

Before I start whining about that, I fling myself down on the mattress, determined to grab a couple hours of sleep. Maybe my sleeping brain will sort what is real from what is merely the shock reverberating through my nerves from— yeah—going down with the ship this morning.

I tell myself that whatever parts of this are still real when I wake up, I'll deal with them then.

Seconds tick off, endlessly. As I go in and out of dark states that aren't sleep, I hear Dad tossing on the sofa. At one point in the night, it sounds like he's opening the window. At another, the creaking floor overhead jolts me awake. Ollie and her parents are restless—they must be opening their windows too. I hear, or maybe I dream, Dad waking up, shivering, dragging shut the window above the sofa, pulling on his sweatshirt. I dream, or imagine, Jennifer upstairs, feeling around for blankets in a dark closet, finding one, tucking it around Ollie.

Twice during the hours of full-blown sleeplessness, I dig my phone out from under my pillow and bleed another drop of salt water from its ports. I want to make sure that the photo of my mom will still materialize on the home screen. The first time I check, it appears. As my finger traces the bracelet on her wrist, I drift off. Hours later when I check again, the screen glows like a near-dead flashlight, deepening the gloom of my bunk cave. I watch Mom's face pixelate and fragment. It's grotesque.

Finally, I must have fallen asleep for real. I must have felt the damp cold seep into the house, pulled the covers around my neck, and curled my body into a ball.

That's the state I am in when the spring on the screen door thrums and my left eye opens a slit. Through the grey predawn light, it observes Stuart close the door behind him as quietly as possible. He's shivering from the dampness that permeates everything and—he's coming over to my bunk.

Stuart stoops to pick something up off the floor—my sketchbook. He places it gently on the blanket beside me.

The next time my eye opens, Stuart is crouching in the sitting room, building a fire in the wood stove. Dad startles awake and mumbles words I can't make out.

"Sorry. It's freezing out there," Stuart replies in a husky whisper.

"No problem…yeah…good idea," Dad says, clearing his throat. He pulls his blanket tighter and slides along the length of the sofa, closer to the stove. One after the other,

Jennifer, Mark and Ollie descend the ladder-stairs, which can't be easy when you're wrapped in blankets. They huddle together on the floor next to the stove and fall asleep.

I'm awake just enough to realize that I'm freezing too. Curling up and making a hood for my head out of the blanket fails to generate heat. I force myself awake, but not one brain cell more than what's needed to climb out from under my clammy blanket…stumble through the frigid kitchen…seek warmth in the sitting room…and creep onto the sofa. There, I slump against Dad, a parasite on his body heat.

The second insanely huge temperature change in a little more than 24 hours transforms us into a restless den of hibernating animals. In August.

DAY ONE, AEC

STUART IS THE FIRST TO BE UP, out, and greeting Day One, AEC. Before it ends, he will give me a full account of how, for him, today started "promising enough."

He opens his eyes and finds himself in a sandwich of sleeping family members. The fire has died, and incredibly, the weather is back to being August hot both inside the house and out. After freeing himself from the tangle of bodies, Stuart comes into the kitchen, where he sees me back in the bunk and dead asleep.

He insists that he tried not to notice my open sketchbook while he was lacing up his running shoes. But it was right there on the edge of my bed and, he admits, he failed. This new diagram was impossible for him to ignore because, as he will put it to me later, "It was way weirder than your other ones."

Soon after, when he's on the beach and trying to find his zone, he can't get the drawing he saw out of his head. He figures that's what made him miss the moment that everything around him changed: the wind stopped; the waves flattened; the gulls floated in abnormal silence.

Meanwhile, back in the keeper's house, for me the day has begun less promisingly. Sunlight and the morning racket of birds finally reach the depths of the bunk-cave. It's taking a lot of effort to wake up, and I slowly become aware of the fact that I'm soaked in sweat.

I kick off the blanket and go to rub my eyelids open. But my hands have locked themselves onto my open sketchbook. I blink into the beam of sunlight that spotlights a new drawing that sprawls across two pages. I have no memory of making it. If there is such a thing as sleep drawing, I seem to have done it.

Later, when Stuart and I debrief each other about the morning's events, I can only agree with him: this new drawing is far more disturbed than the ones in my old sketchbook. The longer my eyes run along the tortured tangle of lines and the more awake I become, the more unsettling the drawing grows. Yet, I can't shake the feeling that answers might be hiding in its labyrinth. But which of my bazillion questions am I supposed to ask it?

My bunk cave is stifling. I haven't stopped sweating. I climb out. On my way to the door, I pass by the sitting room where bundled lumps lie on the floor. In their sleep, they stir and peel off layers of blankets.

I shuffle out of the main house, grateful for the fact that no one is awake enough to behold my wretched appearance. I aim for the picnic table, eyes squinched against the dazzling sunlight. Sitting down with my sketchbook, I resume investigation of the drawing that my nocturnal self has left behind.

The marks emanate an energy that, even in daylight, tends toward ominous. This triggers a fresh rush of stress hormones—which proves to be motivating because, as I ride them out, I remember what I told myself last night: Whatever was still real when I woke up this morning, I would deal with it then.

Well, this is then.

I clutch the marker tighter and vow to put an end to the questions that have my sense of reality hanging by a thread. Leaning into the sketchbook, I burn the following words into the blank page: *Today, I will find out: 1) what is wrong with my family, 2) what is wrong with me, that those college tours I'm going on next week feel like they're meant for some other lifetime, and—yeah—3) what strange force has taken over my drawings?*

Great. Something to steer by.

Stepping away from the picnic table in triumph, I stretch my arms wide in the morning sun's noon-like warmth.

I savor my newfound sense of clarity for all of ten seconds, right up until the background din of squawking sea gulls goes mute. I drop my arms and look around. Something is drawing sound away from our island. All sound—except for the sound-feeling. It is pulsing in from the northeast just like it did last night.

I turn slowly toward the sensation. It swirls around me. I can tell that its intensity has grown overnight. So has its anguish. But there is no figuring out what it could be. Nothing about it is familiar or recognizable.

I resign myself to adding one more question to the "what is going on?" list. Turning back to the table, I print in even larger letters: *4) what is making the sound-feeling?*

I figure I might as well get right on number four. Inhaling a long breath, then letting it out, I put down the marker, gather up my senses and turn to the northeast.

Vibrations shudder up the back of my neck. I can't say why, but something about that makes me pivot, slowly, until I face due east.

Out of the glare of sunrise, a formation of soundless, low-flying birds streams toward our island. The rush of air passing over their black wings rips open the silence. Their long necks slash past, yards above the roof of the house. I twist to watch them whirl and push north into the distance. They shrink to black dots, then disappear.

Suffocating silence returns. I hold my breath. There's something more. I plant my feet firmly on the grass before I dare to turn west. When I do, I'm standing face to face with a steel gray battleship of a shelf cloud. Massed into an angular wedge and distinctly drawn against the blue-white sky, it could be the masterwork of a diabolical architect. It could be the mother ship from any number of sci-fi movies. It could be a bad dream.

But it is nothing that mundane. It is—unheard of. And it is here to deliver to East Ledge Islanders our first life-rattling event of Day One, AEC.

"Oh. God," I mutter to no one, and I run for the house.

Later, Stuart and I will calculate that, at this very moment, he was deeply absorbed in vaulting off of a high boulder while executing an easy-going 90 degree turn. He'll tell me that, as he continued on his freerun, he started to think about my drawing again. And that is when the blackness of the shelf cloud entered his peripheral vision and exploded into his awareness.

He says he "skidded to an inelegant stop." I believe him, even though I can't picture Stuart skidding or doing anything else in a way you would call inelegant. He doesn't know where to move next. From the look on his face when he tells me this, it's obvious he is not used to *that*, either.

So, there we have Stuart, frozen in place on the beach, while back at the main house, we've got me and Dad dragging the mattress off my bunk and jamming its bulk against the kitchen window on the cloud-facing side of the house.

Mark rushes through rooms, closing more windows.

"Mark? Where is Stuart?" Jennifer shouts, pulling Ollie away from the door.

Ollie's eyes are huge, and she's asking, "Do we have a basement?"

Stuart slams open the screen door and bursts into the kitchen. "Get into the lighthouse, now!" he shouts.

He grabs Ollie's arm and propels her through the doorway.

In our collective dash across the lawn, the door of the lighthouse tower taunts us like a receding horizon. We take turns stealing glimpses of the churning, soot-black cloud as if, by not looking it in the eye, we can make ourselves invisible.

At last we throw ourselves through the lighthouse door and cram together under the spiral of iron steps. Stuart and I wrap our bodies as shields around Ollie.

The total absence of wind right now is beyond eerie. Whatever field of force is out there, it is concentrating its strength into a vertical press—squeezing the entire atmosphere above our island downward into the lighthouse and against our chests.

Then, it releases.

My ears pop, and pop again. I hear straight-line wind strafing the walls. Nano-bullets of sand pelt the tower's porthole windows and eat away bits of glass. High up the lighthouse stairs, window panes smash. Shards of glass and fist-sized hailstones cascade down the metal steps and shatter on the cement floor around us.

But still, there is no rain. Not a drop.

The lighthouse door explodes open. Balls of hail pile up at the doorstep. Dune grasses whip and flay.

Stuart jumps to pull the door closed but a violent updraft slaps him back and then climbs the tower to blow out even more windows.

With that, suddenly, it is done with us.

The swinging lighthouse door frames the butt end of the shelf cloud as it passes overhead and scuds eastward.

Gingerly, we untangle ourselves from each other's grasps. Checking for injuries, we turn up multiple bruises, but nothing worse.

Not looking forward to what we might find outside, we file out of the tower one by one. Incredibly, the sun is already breaking through the ragged remnants of the storm. Its morning cheerfulness mocks the gravity of what just went down, the same way the sudden calm did after the rogue wave.

But no one makes light of the torn-up shingles and lethal ice-rocks of hail that litter the grounds. The wood stove's metal chimney points eastward now, as if to say, "It went that way." But that's not funny either. The few trees that have been trying to make it on this rocky island dangle partially severed limbs. The poles that hold the weather instruments teeter at dizzy angles. Window frames on the main house gape open where ice balls drove through their panes.

I hear tapping sounds and look up to see that the satellite dish is swinging from its cable and rapping against the red bricks of the radio shack.

We pinch our noses and force ourselves to yawn, struggling to bring the pressure in our heads back to normal. Through the crackling in my ear, I hear Dad's emergency manager voice saying, "We should check the systems in the house."

Jennifer sets Ollie free from a protective mom clutch and joins Mark in trailing Dad into the keeper's house.

Stuart puts his arm around Ollie and looks over at me.

"You knew it was coming," he says. He's not even trying to hide the expression that is on his face, the one that says he knows my secret: it wasn't a shipwreck that brought me here—it was a flying saucer.

My heart hasn't stopped pounding in the wake of the storm's violence, and Stuart is not helping.

"OK, maybe I *did* know something was coming. But like I told you—I don't know what that means. Besides, how do *you* know what I know?"

"She knew *what* was coming? What did you know, Kally?" Ollie asks.

"Remember me teaching you about how spacecraft have tell-tales?" Stuart asks Ollie.

"Yeah," she says. "That's those indicators on the space ship's dashboard. They tell the pilot about conditions they need to track or do something about."

"Right," he says. "Kally's new drawing is doing that. It's a tell-tale."

"Crazy," Ollie says.

I scowl at Stuart in self-defense, even as I struggle to recall details of this morning's drawing. Because, it *did* know something. I remember studying it at the picnic table…just before the shelf cloud appeared…because I was trying to understand—

A shadow slashes across our faces. Our edgy nerves fire and we recoil. A few feet above our heads, the outstretched wings of a prehistorically large bird glide through a graceful, 360 degree turn.

"A pelican!" Ollie squeals.

It's magnificent. It floats lower and lower, then tucks and dives below the rim of the cliff.

The three of us run to the drop-off. In the water below, wooden planks that used to be East Ledge Island's pier jostle and bang against the stripped pilings. The ocean rowboat has beached its aluminum self halfway up the sand cliff, where it pokes out, partially buried.

And then, I spot what is left of *Home* lying wrecked against the beach steps. The whirlwind ripped her from her anchor, freed her from the sandbar, and hurled her to shore.

The pelican glides inches above sea. Against its grey foam, she traces a brilliant white flight path the shape of a half-moon before she sets down, handsomely, on *Home*'s broken hull.

Just when I'm feeling grateful that there is still such a thing as a calm after the storm, high-pitched hissing sounds rush up the beach from the south. At first, I take it to be the electric zing of a storm-rattled, stowaway cicada. But the buzzing ramifies into a chest-pounding staccato.

We leap back from the edge.

The pelican springs up from *Home.*

A quarter of a mile down the beach from us, a chunk of the island the size of a football field sings with friction as it sheers and slumps. Then it simply—gives way.

Stuart and I grab Ollie by her shirt and pull her with us into a panicked retreat from the bluff. When we finally dare to stop and look behind us, the first thing we see is the pelican, flying east with all of her strength.

"Come back," Ollie implores, in a tiny voice.

Ollie sprints toward the main house with Stuart and me at her heels. "Mom! Dad!" she shouts. "The whole side of the island fell off, and that storm blew a pelican all the way here from—"

Ollie flings open the screen door and we burst into the kitchen.

"Don't come in!" Jennifer shouts, performing the universal halt sign with both hands.

The windows over the sink are blown in. Shattered glass covers the kitchen floor. Mark and Jennifer are stepping carefully to avoid the shards.

Mark makes it over to the light switch and flips it up and down. No electricity. Dad is in the sitting room searching for something. He finds it: the AM radio. It's in pieces. Jennifer picks the keeper's list of instructions up off the floor.

"Want me to read the part about the backup generator?" she asks, stoically.

After an hour of cleaning up glass and other storm debris, we gather basic breakfast food and carry it out of the kitchen chaos to the picnic table. It feels slightly safer out here. At least, it does until Ollie fills the parents in with details about how "one whole side of the island fell off," and how she can't wait to show that to them after we eat.

I brush broken shingles, melting hail, and blown sand off one of the benches and sit down with my sketchbook. It took a while to find it. The wind wedged it between the kitchen wall and the refrigerator. I pull a splinter of window glass out from between its pages and try to smooth their wrinkles.

Dad tinkers with the broken window frame he has laid out at one end of the table. At the other end, Mark performs exploratory surgery on the AM radio.

Over near the wind-bent weather instruments, Stuart has been pacing in that oh so fluid way of his while taking bites from his un-toasted bread. It's clear that he's turning something over in his mind.

"Maybe we should go," he says eventually.

"Yeah? Where?" my dad snaps.

That sounded rude. He's never rude.

"I don't want to go," Ollie informs Stuart, her nose buried yet again in the weather log. "There's a NOAA weather station here."

"And it's broken," Stuart shoots back, pointing at the instrument poles. "Just like everything else."

"So? We'll fix it," Ollie fires right back. She closes the log and clutches it to her chest.

Jennifer picks bits of glass out of the sand beneath the picnic table. "It's still the most beautiful place I've ever been," she says.

"This isn't exactly a vacation anymore," Stuart points out. "Plus, everyone has other places they need to be."

"You mean *you* do." Ollie scowls at her brother.

I sense an opportunity to offer Stuart support. It's the least I can do for the guy who saved my life. Besides, Stuart has dared to speak of the elephant at the picnic. And after this morning's events, I'm fully back to wanting to discuss the reality meat grinder we seem to be living in.

I close my sketchbook and stand up from the table.

"I think Stuart is right, don't you, Dad? As soon as we tell the keeper about the storm damage and all of the other strange things that have been happening out here, he'll *have* to send somebody out to get us. For free, probably."

Stuart sends me an appreciative nod and we scan the three parents for signs of agreement. But suddenly, not one of them is willing to meet our eyes.

Mark dives back into the broken radio. "There's no way to email or call the keeper or anybody else until that satellite dish gets fixed," he says.

Stuart's face hardens with frustration, and he presses, "Why do you sound so relieved about that?"

But for now, Mark is spared the task of answering his son. The whine of a high-speed motor is piercing our island bubble.

CHANGING

, we must make one pitiful tableau of a seriously shipwrecked, storm-shaken blended family. We are straight out of a summer Disney movie gone very, very wrong.

I'm not sure where to look—at my first, sickening, closeup view of *Home*'s broken body, half buried in the sand at my feet; the shambles of undone earth that used to be one of the southeastern bluffs of this island; or this guy in front of us, dressed in a camouflage wet suit, manfully straddling his exhaust-spitting jet boat, shouting to be heard above the unnecessary din of his own making.

"The keeper sent me out here to check on you. That was one excellent storm," he says.

He revs his motor to keep the surf from pushing him into what is left of the pier pilings. It's obvious that his energy is dialed up, just like his motor, otherwise, he could just beach his jet and talk to us like a normal person.

"What we caught here was nothing—just the edge," he says. "It messed up the whole East Coast."

I grab my dad's arm. "Dad!"

"What's that about the East Coast?" Dad shouts.

"Portland. Boston. Jersey. New York. D.C. And way south of that. Chaos. Power's out everywhere. Flooding. Wall to wall wind damage. People cut off from each other. Closed Interstates. Crazy shit."

"Derecho," Ollie says, and notes it in her log.

"Dad," I say again, unable to control the wavering in my voice.

"She'll be OK, Kally. She's with people who have planned for things like this."

What is he talking about? Is this the *even more* he couldn't tell me yesterday?

"She's what? What people?" I shout in his ear. "And what do you mean, 'things like this'? *What* did they plan for?" But Dad acts like he doesn't hear me.

Mark calls across the water, "Nothing like that was in the forecast."

"You're joking, right?" the guy shouts back. "They haven't gotten the weather right around here for months." He lets go a jeering laugh.

"The derecho blew a pelican here," Ollie shouts.

The guy slides his sun goggles up onto his helmet and looks at us, then *Home*, like we're lab specimens in some marine survival experiment he's come to check on.

"Everything OK here?"

Mark fills him in. "Broken windows, shingles blown off. Satellite dish is damaged. We have no power—the cable from the mainland is out. But the backup generator is running. The pier is gone, as you can see."

"effin' lucky," the guy says.

"When is the keeper coming to get us?" Stuart calls out.

"A water spout took out the harbor. Most of the rest of the town too. Not one civilian boat made it. Coast Guard saw it coming. They rode it out."

"We need to be off of here by Saturday," Stuart calls back.

"Coast Guard's up to their necks. But they should be able to make it out here by then," the guy yells.

I can see a wave of relief run through Stuart's body as he says to himself, "OK. Great. That's good."

The guy revs his engine's propeller.

"Wait," I interject. "My mom. She's in New York. We don't know if she's OK."

"You and everybody else needs to reach somebody," he says while removing a strip of seaweed that got caught in his cuff.

Was that supposed to make me feel better? I turn to Dad, but he's not even listening. He's pacing alongside what's left of *Home*.

The guy guns the engine again. "I gotta get back to town. Place is all torn up. My house included. I'll let them know you're still here. Crazy lucky." He laughs again, which, for a thousand reasons, really ticks me off. He points the boat away from the beach and the waterjet shoots a violent arc of sea foam high into the air.

"No! Wait!" I shout. But his boat accelerates to at least 50 mph and screams away.

"Hear that?" Stuart turns to his dad. "We'll be on the mainland by Saturday. I'll make it back in time." He pivots to Jennifer. "Sorry about before. It's just that, when I thought I would miss the start of internship—anyway, I'll finish my run and then I'll help you fix things at the house."

Stuart takes off running and calls over his shoulder, "We'll have our vacation—we've got almost a whole week left."

I glare at his back. It's great that he's going to keep his date with Houston. But an entire coast of the continent is messed up and I don't know if my mom is—

"We need to tell him, Mark," I hear Jennifer say under her breath, "so that he has time to—"

"Yes, I know," Mark says. He offers to carry Ollie's logbook for her and, as she relates everything she knows about derechos, he and Jennifer each take one of her hands and they head up the steps together.

My jealous anger at Stuart slams into reverse. I wish I could take back that snarky glare I just burned into his back. He's not the only one who hasn't been thinking beyond his own life. And I'm not the only one whose parents have been keeping something from them. But at least Mark and Jennifer are *thinking* about telling their son what the big secret is. There's no telling *what* Dad is thinking. He has gone all silent again, pretending to study our wrecked sailboat while his eyes are seeing something else entirely.

"Dad? What did you mean just now? Who is Mom with? Where is she *really*?"

He clenches his jaw muscles and turns away from *Home*. "We'll talk, Kally. Later."

He starts toward the beach stairs. I stumble through the sand after him.

"Didn't you hear what that guy said about New York?

The Harts can wait until Saturday to get picked up if they want to. But we have to get off this island now so we can find Mom." I stop at the steps and call after him. "Dad! Why aren't you even *trying* to do that?"

"Later." He disappears over the top of the steps.

Why "later?" What's wrong with now? I want to run after him and make him tell me all of it. But I feel trapped and crushingly heavy. I'm facing straight into the wind, stalled and unable to maneuver. When that happens to a boat, sailors call it being "caught in irons." I never knew a person's life could get caught in irons.

I turn from the steps, only to confront the wreckage of *Home*. Getting wrenched off the sandbar and slammed into the beach has left her with a refrigerator-sized hole in her side. I can't pull my eyes away from it.

Churning out one grim thought after another, my mind rubs salt in its wounds. *That hole is right where her heart would be if she were a sea creature. I will never work her mainsail again or feel her tug and skitter when she finds her groove in the wind and water.*

I try to imagine how Dad could fix any of that. But I can't. Anger and confusion about his failure to communicate burn in my face. I need to move. I need to get out of irons and put the wind at my back again.

I pull myself away from *Home* and look south. The thin strip of beach narrows, gradually, to nothing. A wisp of fog floats between me and that nothing. I set out for it. Maybe a walk will help me make sense of the last 24 hours.

Thick mats of storm-churned sea foam toss in the surf to my left. On my right, driftwood and snapped trees project at sharp angles out of the slumped earth of the landside.

The things that have just happened across planet Earth

and in my own family are supposed to happen hardly ever, much less all in one day. But here I am, walking through the proof of their rampage. The storm threw up heaps of plastic trash, leaving neon-colored pockmarks on the cliff's face. Along its shoulder, boulders lean from their dissolving perches, threatening to let loose and flatten everything below. Meanwhile, in my brain, fear neurons fire at will about my family.

Maybe I'm overreacting. I decide to take inventory.

One titanic rogue wave.

One *Home* wrecking colossus of a downburst.

One embarrassing shipwreck off a lighthouse island inhabited by a pleasant suburban family that is just trying to have fun.

One emergency physical extraction of me out of the ocean by an aspiring NASA astronaut—make that—flight controller.

One parade of three whacked-out weather seasons across one night.

One swarm of ghost birds.

One lightning rod and one finger set ablaze by St. Elmo.

One reality-bending roll cloud whirlwind (aka Ollie's "derecho") that knocks out our power, windows and satellite dish in what was, according to a twitchy boatercycle dude, a mere local swat from a meteorological monster fest that partied its way down half the continent.

One pathetically lost but resilient pelican who gets blown to New England from…Florida?

Three (and counting) family-busting secrets that my dad and mom co-conspired to keep from me.

One ongoing loss of contact with the entire rest of the

world except for the aforementioned boatercycle dude.

One missing mother. Mine.

I can't let myself think about that last one for more than one second.

I'm sure there is more. (Did I mention the quaking sandslide?) But I stop, because I've come up against the camel humps of uprooted dune grasses that plowed down the cliff this morning. The sand in the mounds they created is too loose to walk in. I take my shoes off, skirt the barrier by wading through the waves that are coming ashore, then continue on.

Back on course toward the SUV-sized rocks that break up the beach ahead, I bet myself that a glacier pushed those rocks and the whole rest of the island out here from some place in Maine. If the internet even existed on East Ledge Island, I'd look that up.

I'm considering whether a glacier counts as a force field, when I find myself at the wall of boulders. They are twice my height. Several perch on top of each other. Others nestle against one another, separated by narrow corridors of dusky dampness.

I thread my body between two slate-colored walls of stone. The cave-like gap is cool and refreshing until it turns claustrophobic. Pivoting sideways, I squeeze on for a few yards more.

Suddenly, I'm out of the passageway and poised on a glistening dome of smooth, exposed rock. It curves downward in a gentle slope for a dozen yards before plunging into the sea.

The sun is brilliant here at the southern tip of our island. In front of me, the ocean expands away in directions I haven't been able to see until now. While, in my mind's eye, the entirety of East Ledge Island behind me shrinks to a speck—as if I were looking at it through the wrong end of a telescope.

Waves slide up the dome and slap my feet playfully. Thoughts and feelings about my mom ride in on the silken sheets of water. She is somewhere impossibly far off in the very direction I'm facing. Terrifying movie trailers loop in my head about what could be happening around her—and to her—in the city. The one thing I want in the entire world is to know she is OK.

But I don't know that.

The monotonous rising and falling of the surf is lulling. Too lulling. I turn away from its deception and plunge back into the dank channel between the boulders. I want to put their thick wall between me and all bad news from everywhere.

In no mood to be with anyone, I take my time walking back to the lighthouse. On this pass, the beach cusps at the water's edge catch my eye. In the aftermath of this morning's storm, waves have pushed up delicate ridges of sand and scalloped them into long overlapping curves.

I love beach cusps. They're mysterious. Scientists still don't know what makes them appear. Their best guess—which is so cool—is that these sweet, graceful forms are the traces of long gone storms whose leftover energy is still coming ashore, even today. When conditions are perfect, that lingering energy transforms lapping waves into master sculptors. You could say that beach cusps are the footprints of their own history.

Even in my deteriorating mood, I appreciate how

excellent that is.

I squat and run my finger along the ridge of one of the cusps. It's a precarious spine of a line. The next high tide will wipe it out easily.

Maybe everything that exists, including rogue waves, is a ghost footprint of its own history. Maybe bits of energy left over from winds, waves, temperatures, air pressures—across all the oceans all the way back to when oceans got started—randomly bump into each other. Then, maybe they join forces and continue on their way, stomping their compounding footprint as they go. And there you have it: a rogue wave. Or, a downburst, roll cloud, landslide, continental power outage, or—yeah—a missing mom.

I straighten my back, slap sticky granules of sand off of my hands, and stand up. I've made zero progress on the vow I made this morning. In fact, the knots of confusion are more twisted than ever. And amassing that inventory of recent chaos (which, come to think of it, didn't even include Dad's refusal to talk to me) has left me feeling even worse.

Obliterating sand cusps with each step, I set a fast pace back up the beach, determined to pull myself back on course: find Dad, so we can work on finding Mom, so we can fix my family.

Even from this far away, East Ledge Light dominates the landscape, out-scaling its small perch on the sand cliff. My body might be back on course, but my mind churns wildly as I head toward it. They didn't put a major lighthouse like that out here for nothing. This place is a crossroads of powerful winds and waters with billions of years of history jammed up behind them. Currents get seriously jumbled here. So do rocks of the earth. Maybe lives get scrambled here, too. Maybe if Dad and I weren't on this island, maybe if we were home, maybe—

I spot Stuart a hundred yards ahead, running along the edge of the cliff. He's still on that workout he wanted to finish after the jet boat guy left.

The longer I watch him, the more I realize this is not your usual jogging. Stuart doesn't bother to go around driftwood, beach rocks, trees, or even sand dunes. He heads straight for them instead. He deliberately turns them into his own personalized obstacle course.

I'm brought to a complete stop at the sight of him blasting off on a near vertical run up the face of a rock outcropping, vaulting into the air, spinning a full 360 degrees, and landing like his body is a glider. I could have been watching current flow through wire. It was impressive. And, honestly? It was intimidating. I have never been able to do anything that—directly. Which is probably why, unlike Stuart, I have never been able to dream a dream for my life.

Stuart is fast becoming one big continuous reminder of that.

He catches me watching him and immediately bounds over to the lip of the cliff. Plunging knee deep into the sand, he takes giant steps down the steep wall. Now, he's jogging in my direction in cool-down mode.

I am in no mood for small talk. It's time I tried being *direct* for a change. Staring straight ahead, I resume my tack toward the lighthouse, reciting to myself: *find Dad, so we can work on finding—*

"You OK?" Stuart falls in step beside me and catches his breath.

At least that's not a small talk question. I wonder if Stuart realizes just how much it isn't. Whatever, I cannot let myself get started on how fully un-OK I am.

"I've never seen someone jog the way you do," I say, making small talk.

"It's not jogging. It's freerunning."

Sounds to me like he's feeling just great about that.

"Uh-huh. And freerunning is…?" I ask while I persist on my march up the beach.

"A martial art. It's a sport, too. The whole point is to keep going—no matter what shows up—without breaking anything. Including yourself. When you hit a barrier, you escape it by interacting with it."

Turns out, it's not just NASA that he's into. This freerunning thing makes him out-and-out happy. He wants to share.

"For a few of my friends it's a way of life," he continues. "They live it as their…" His voice trails off.

I glance over at him. I think he's afraid he just came across as the biggest geek ever. That's comforting. Given what he's seen in my sketchbook, and given the "Kally knew a rogue wave was coming" bulletin that Dad broadcast from the bathroom yesterday, I'm sure I've been coming across as a flakey psychic artist wannabe.

"Your friends live freerunning as their…?"

He hesitates, then says, "Philosophy." He looks away.

"Do you?" I ask.

His eyes dart to mine. He checks to see if that was a snarky question. But it wasn't. The first time I saw Stuart through the binoculars, I could tell he was different. Now I'm learning what kind of different he is. Being stranded on a close-to-deserted island with a super athlete astronaut-philosopher is…intriguing.

Stuart looks like he's weighing how much he should reveal about his philosophy of life. But, hey, he's still in that zone of hope he entered when he heard he would be off of East Ledge Island by Saturday. So, he goes for it.

"I freerun because it's a reality check. You have to tune your movements to where you are and what's around you. I like how that makes me—ready."

"Ready for…?"

"Twists and turns. You know, like what's been happening since we landed here." He pulls off his cap and wipes sweat from his eyes.

"And like what happens in space?" I ask, reading the NASA logo on his cap.

"Yeah." He exudes a new surge of self-satisfaction, takes a long breath and scans East Ledge Island. "I thought there'd be no place I could freerun here, but the boulders are better than fire escapes. And that tower is at least a week's worth of technically challenging horizontal wall runs—"

"Uh-huh," I interrupt. I can tell that he has gotten over whatever made him adorably self-conscious a few seconds ago. "Well, I'm not exactly on a family vacation here. So, listen, I could use some help."

"Sure!" Stuart fires back, sounding like he has never been unsure of a thing. "What's up?"

"What's up is, my mother is missing."

"Yeah, that stuff going on with your mom and dad is rough."

I stop in my tracks and plant my feet in the sand.

"Seriously?"

"Small island," he says, attempting a joke. But he's been caught, and he knows it.

"Tiny. And that is why you should *not* listen to the private conversations of the other inhabitants. Or spy on their sketchbooks!"

"The only parts I heard were the ones you and your dad shouted."

I redirect my indignant glare at the sea. Dad and I *were* shouting. Stuart probably wasn't *trying* to eavesdrop.

He takes off a shoe and shakes out a full cup of sand. "My folks had a rough stretch last year. Worst part was, Ollie and I knew something was wrong, but they refused to admit it. So, we withheld all information about ourselves. They caved after two days. Hence—The Pact."

"The Pact," I say, still looking out to sea.

"Yeah. If something is going on with them that could alter the trajectories of our lives, they have to tell us."

"And that's working," I say, flatly.

"Yeah." But he can't help registering the skepticism that is beaming at him from my end of the conversation. "Why?"

"Oh, nothing," I say as unconvincingly as I can.

"No—why did you say 'oh nothing' like that?"

"Maybe because every time you remind your folks you have to get back home for your big date with NASA, they exhibit classic parental avoidance behavior. Like that look on their faces at lunch."

"What do you mean? What look?"

I can tell that Stuart is replaying the failed breakfast conversation of a few hours ago. Even *he* couldn't miss the way Mark and Jennifer dodged his question about why they are relieved to be cut off from the rest of the world. But now, I feel evil. My desire to dent the shiny, streamlined surface of Stuart's spaceship is mean. Still, the way he's zooming into his future at orbital speed, everything happening around him amounts to little more than a blur in his viewport. He's hardly even noticed that, back here on Earth, the rest of us Earthlings are getting the forward motion knocked out of us because things are going more and more out of whack in bigger ways than anyone on this island will take in or admit. *Somebody* has got to clue him in.

But I can't let myself get blown any further off course.

"It's probably just me," I say. "Anyway, can you help me reach my mother?"

"Uh, sure. Reach her how?" Stuart mumbles.

What I said about his parents has him all distracted, and I have to spell it out. "Will you help me fix the satellite dish so I can call my mom, or at least email her?"

"Um, yeah. I'll, uh, meet you up there. In a few minutes."

Stuart takes a step, hesitates, reverses course, then reverses course again. Finally, he heads down the beach in the direction I just came from. But he's not freerunning anymore, he's just plain jogging with a heavy step. Which makes me—yeah—ashamed of myself for being such a jealous jerk about the laser beam lock that he has on his life's dream.

Just as I decide to run after him, I catch sight of Dad. He's come back down to the beach. He's working hard on something I can't make out from here.

Stay the course, I tell myself.

I make a mental note to apologize to Stuart the next chance I get.

WHAT'S ALREADY HERE

 find Dad, so we can work on finding Mom, so we can fix my family. Repeat. Find Dad, so we can work on finding Mom—

As I close in on Dad's worksite, I'm able to make out objects that are strewn across the sand: sail remnants, tangled rope, pulleys, cleats, a broken mast and rudder— plus all sorts of tools that Dad must have hauled down here from one of the service buildings.

"Dad! Stop!" I shout, breaking into a run.

Sweating and on automatic, he's dragging the aluminum rowboat down from where it beached halfway up the cliff.

"You're not fixing *Home*, you're scrapping her!"

"We need a working boat," he says, as he yanks and rakes the rowboat across the sand.

"We do? Why? And what working boat? This?" I say, pointing to *Home*'s scattered remains. Suddenly, I understand what he is up to. "Oh. No," I say, "we are not putting out to sea in a kludged together rowboat-sailboat!"

I cringe at how that sounded like I'm boss of everyone. But I can see that it rattled Dad's autopilot, so I keep going.

"Look, Dad, this is not the project we should be doing anymore. We should be finding out if Mom is OK. You heard that guy from town. Who knows what's happening back there? Finding Mom is what matters now—not fixing boats."

I reach for the rope, the one he's been using to drag the rowboat. He lets me take it.

"Dad. What's wrong with you?"

He walks over to the broken hull of *Home* and sinks down onto it. I've never seen my dad act this way. Defeated. A victim of the emergency—not its manager.

"I didn't build *Home* for what the ocean has become, Kally," he says. "I knew I shouldn't bring her out here anymore."

Struggling to understand, I look at the ocean. "What do you mean? What has it become?"

"I knew it when I asked you to take this trip. But I didn't want to give up."

"Give up on what?"

"Kally, I nearly got you killed."

I drop the rope I've been holding, push through the sand to *Home*, and sit next to him.

"OK," I say, through a deep breath. "You know that talk you promised we would have later? This is later."

He looks at his hands. "Yesterday, you asked me where that rogue wave came from. It—and everything else that's been happening—it's coming from everywhere." He picks up a broken batten from *Home*'s sail and drives it into the sand at his feet. "No, that's wrong. It's not *coming*, Kally. It's already here."

I try to stop my brain from echoing "it's already here." But the inventory I just made of Day One, AEC, ticker tapes through my mind. I recognize instantly what my dad is saying. This is what I have been wanting to talk about with him and everybody else. *It's already here.* Except, now that he has said it, my emotions have assumed the fetal position. All I want is to protect myself, my mom, my dad—everything and everybody—from what is *already here.*

Denial has been our default strategy for so long—it is as good as hard-wired. And it wins yet again when I mutter, "But, that's not, that's not for sure…"

"It *is* for sure," Dad says firmly. "It has been for a long time. First, we tried to stop it, then we tried to plan for it. But that was just as useless. No, worse, it was a lie. And my job in emergency management did nothing but feed the lie."

He stands up and kicks divots into the sand. "There's no managing this. All of the work your mother and I did these past 20 years?" My head swivels to follow him as he circles *Home.* "The organizing, the lobbying, the policy proposals— the art she creates about the environment? None of it made a dent. Everything is changing too much, too fast. What your mom continues to insist on doing is a waste of time."

It's frightening to hear him say these things. But they are not news to me. At some point, I don't remember when, an awareness of what he just said worked its way into me. It has been living inside of me on a level way deeper than knowing.

I pull myself up from *Home* and walk to the water's edge. This is worse than opening my eyes when I was eight feet under our turtled boat. At least then, I knew what to do. I had to swim toward air and light. Or—was it Dad that I was swimming toward?

I turn from the ocean and watch him, sitting on *Home* again, folding and unfolding a fragment of her sail, over and over. I refocus on the one scrap of Day One, AEC that I might possibly get my head around—the one part that might be fixable. If Dad and I work together, the way we problem-solve snags we hit on sailing trips, we might be able to fix the piece that is about our family.

In the gentlest voice I can muster, I say, "You told Mom her life's work is a useless waste of time? On the phone? I'm not surprised that she's mad at you."

"That's not why she's mad. She's mad because she thinks I gave up. That's the real reason she went to New York."

My stunned silence steals his attention away from the scrap of sail. When he sees the confusion in my eyes, he takes a deep breath. "Your mother didn't go to the city to install her art. She went to join a coalition of artists who are mobilizing to—"

"Mobilizing? What artists? She never told *me*—"

"I was going to tell you everything on this trip."

"Were you!" My self-defense mechanisms kick back in, big time. "So *that's* what this trip is? Your management plan for disclosing a boatload of family secrets—days before I'm supposed to get on a bus and go tour colleges in the name of the dream future I still haven't dreamt?"

"Kally, how could your mother and I tell you the things we couldn't even tell ourselves?"

If that's how it *really* was, he's got a point. But it doesn't calm the anxiety storm that is building in my chest. And I'm already reassessing the last few months of tension-filled family life in light of his confession.

"What else couldn't you guys tell me?" I ask. "That we moved out of our perfectly fine lives in the city and went to live in the woods because, *it's already here*? That you decided our family needed to be—what? What are we, now that it's already here? Drop outs? Anarchists? Preppers?" I pace a tight circle. "No wonder I don't have a reason to get on that college tour bus. How *could* I dream a dream for my future? My future is *already*—"

"I don't have answers for you, Kally. I don't know what we should be now. And even if I did, it wouldn't make a difference."

I stop pacing. "So, you *did* give up." It's not an accusation. It's just that, I'm feeling my future dissolve into landslides of sand—years and years of them.

"I'm not sure what I've done," Dad says. "I woke up, I suppose. I looked at it straight on."

"Well, whatever you did, to Mom it looks like you gave up on what she does. Don't you get it? Mom believes you gave up on *her*, who she *is*."

Dad mulls that over as if I have said something useful. But he is too spent to make anything of it. The sight of him frozen on *Home*'s torn hull becomes unbearable.

"You know what?" I ask. "We're in irons. But we know how to deal with that. It's one of the first things you taught me, remember? We have to be patient. We have to wait until the wind blows us backward. Because, that's the only way to heel to the weather and get our boat moving forward again. We can't escape from irons without going backward first."

Dad stirs, and I will into action every tattered scrap of energy I have.

"Dad, I think you should keep fitting this rowboat with what is left of *Home*. You're right—it's not safe to be on an island without a working craft." I point up the beach steps. "I'm going topside to help Stuart. We need to fix the satellite dish so we can contact Mom. As soon as we know she's OK, you have to heel to the weather and tell her you did not give up on her—or on you two together."

Like I said—boss of everyone. Except, I'm about to burst out crying. I quickly turn away and commence an emphatic march up the beach steps.

Then, with leg muscles burning, I continue to tramp on across the lighthouse grounds, where the out-of-joint havoc sprung by this morning's storm startles me all over again.

The meteorological marvel that kicked off today and pinned us under the lighthouse stairs has a name. Ollie declared that it shall be known and recorded in her weather log as: *St. Elmo's Whirlwind.*

Stuart and I turned up a soldering gun in the bottom of a box of ham radio gear. But it was impossible to work in the shack. Too much broken window glass. So, we ran an extension cord from the generator to the picnic table.

Now, we are hunched over the damaged satellite dish like a couple of Drs. Frankenstein. Stuart is showing me how to solder the dish's severed arteries back together. I'm so elated by the prospect of making contact with my mom, I keep melting too much metal.

At the other end of the table, Mark and Jennifer have

started the charcoal grill in preparation for cooking a frighteningly tall stack of burgers. Because, how long can the propane fridge keep wheezing like that? Besides, all of us are starved.

Everyone seems relieved to be doing something other than worrying about what the jet boat guy said is happening on the mainland.

I keep checking the beach stairs for signs of Dad. All that does is impair my soldering technique further. For his part, Stuart can't stop looking up from our task to eye his parents.

"Thanks for telling me—you know," he says under his breath.

While we were setting up the soldering gun, I apologized three times to Stuart. The unkind way I informed him that his parents were harboring a secret was—yeah—unkind. I'm grateful that he's not holding it against me.

"No need to thank me," I say. "I've been there."

Stuart turns back to the patient on the picnic table and mutters, "What is up with them, anyway?"

"I'll make sure my dad and I give you guys some space tonight."

Ollie runs up and says, "Here's the paint stuff I found in the shack."

"Thanks, Ollie."

As I take the brush and jar of paint, Dad finally appears. He holds a steady course across the grounds to the picnic table. It looks like he has wind in his sail and could manage anything that is still manageable around here.

When I turn back to soldering, I feel my face relax, at last, into a smile.

"Now sit down for one minute, Ollie, and eat slowly,"

Jennifer says, passing a burger to Ollie.

Dad joins us and gives my shoulder a reassuring squeeze. "We have a boat," he says. "It might not be seaworthy, but it's tidal pool worthy for sure."

I reach up and put my arm around his waist. "Stuart thinks we'll be on email soon," I say.

Dad nods. He swings his leg over the bench and sits in front of the broken window frame that he was fixing when we heard the jet boat coming. But before he can start in on it, Mark places an obscenely huge burger next to him.

"Things have been so over the top," Mark says, "I haven't had the chance to ask. What do you do when you're not sailing?"

Through a mouthful of burger, Dad says, "Carpentry and home repairs. We moved to a small town in southern Maine two months ago. There's always something to fix."

"This place must feel like home, then," Mark says, gesturing at the battered grounds strewn with storm debris.

Dad is a master carpenter and the best sailor in the world, but that is only the beginning. Which is why I say, "We used to live in New York City. They gave Dad a medal for what he did during the last hurricane."

"It wasn't a medal," Dad protests.

"He used to run the Emergency Management Office for all five boroughs," I say, and sit back to savor my moment of payback. I haven't forgotten the "Kally knew the wave was coming" announcement that Dad made from behind the bathroom door.

"I didn't run it," Dad protests again.

Mark looks up from the second round of burgers he is flipping at the grill. "You worked for the EMO? My firm did data analysis for your outfit. I finalized the estimates for storm surges up the sound."

Dad pushes the last bits of burger into his mouth. "Yeah, one of those models nearly got it right."

I know Dad meant it to be a compliment, but Mark looks deflated. He stares down at the charring meat in front of him and says, "I'm not sure getting it right is even possible anymore. Unless your forecast is: 'whatever happens, it will not be what this or any other forecast says it will be.'"

"You just needed a vacation," Jennifer says. She takes the burger flipper out of Mark's hand and scrapes under the sizzling meat.

"It will take more than a vacation," Mark says. "We rely on data that are getting more counterproductive with each day. Tomorrow's weather, next week's air quality, next year's fresh water tables—we base forecasts about those things on how they behaved the last couple of centuries. But conditions then were far from what they are now. We're throwing darts in the dark at moving targets."

Mark drops East Ledge Island's last two burger patties onto the grill. As they sizzle, I'm thinking that, finally, we're getting somewhere. Someone has talked more than two seconds about the *important* things.

Dad pats my shoulder and declares, "You should hire Kally."

"Dad," I hiss in that way that means "*please stop.*" Why do I always forget that I'm the one who loses these payback games of ours? And why is he steering the subject away from what is important?

Stuart looks at me through the curl of solder smoke rising between us. "Tell my folks how you knew the rogue wave was coming," he says.

Him too? I lean into the maze of satellite dish wires and melt another dollop of solder.

Jennifer sets the tattered burger she dislodged from the grill on the table next to me. "Kally, was your dad right? Did you really know—?"

I could act like I didn't hear the question, just like I did in the kitchen yesterday. But I can see that won't work twice. Letting out a long sigh, I set the soldering gun on the table and wipe my hands on my pants.

"Despite what everybody keeps saying, I did not *know* that a rogue wave was coming."

"Then what *did* you know?" Stuart asks.

"I guess…I saw the pattern change…so, I looked to see why."

"What pattern?" Mark asks.

"The pattern we were sailing inside of," I say.

I can tell no one gets what I'm talking about. Who can blame them? But now, they're all looking at me, expecting me to explain things I don't understand myself. I can see they won't stop asking until I fail to explain it once again.

"The direction that the waves are going in, their speed and size, whether they're lined up or overrunning each other—all of that makes a pattern on the water. And *that* makes a pattern in *Home*'s movements. I saw the pattern shift around *Home*. I felt it in how she was moving. Everything surrounding us was starting to change into— something else."

"But rogue waves don't belong to *any* pattern." Mark places a blackened burger on a bun and hands it to Ollie. "They're what *breaks* a pattern. No program designed to simulate irregular waves can read a small patch of ocean and determine a rogue wave is coming."

"She's not saying she did," Stuart corrects his dad. "She's saying she felt the pattern change." Stuart turns towards me and says, "But I don't believe that the *pattern* is what changed. I think it was *you* that changed. Something in you picked up a phase shift and—

Ollie's face lights up. "You mean, like when the Emperor of the Galaxy says, 'there is a great disturbance in the Force?'" Turns out, Ollie does a wicked imitation of the Emperor.

Stuart smiles. "Close."

Again, I notice how I notice each time Stuart smiles.

Mark is outright scrutinizing me now, like I'm a data set he is trying to interpret.

"If Stuart is right, Kally, and you saw—or 'picked up'—a pattern change, then you did what no algorithm can do." He opens his mouth to take a bite, then puts the burger down on the plate. "Now that nearly every Earth system is going rogue, what I'm trained to do is as useless as our data is. The fact is, I have become dangerous. My models make me—and everyone else—think that I actually know what's happening when I don't. *All* the patterns are shifting, and new ones haven't had time to develop. We have nothing to go on. It's all too new and too fast."

"So *that* is what has been bothering you," Jennifer says.

Stuart sets the soldering gun on the table, hard.

"So much for The Pact."

"What pact?" my dad asks innocently, biting into his second burger.

"The pact my family promised to operate under. The one

about how we would always tell each other the important stuff." Stuart steps away from the table and randomly gathers up broken shingles that he tosses into sloppy piles. "You know, like how you think your life's work is a threat to the very people you're trying to help. Or, why I'm the only one worried about how being stuck out here like this puts me on a trajectory that will miss the start of my internship!"

I guess that talk Stuart was waiting to have with his parents is happening now.

Jennifer raises her eyebrows at Mark and says, "Mark?"

"Fair enough, Stuart." Mark wipes his mouth with a paper towel and tucks in his shirt. "There *is* something we need to discuss. Your mom and I felt that, this week, out here, would be a good time and place—"

"For a vacation, right? That's what you *said* this was."

"Stuart, sit down a minute," Mark says.

"I'd rather not."

"He hardly ever sits," Ollie observes through a mouthful of chips.

"We need to discuss your internship, Stuart." Jennifer chews on her lip.

"Yeah. I start next week."

"No. You don't," Mark says.

Gut punched, Stuart falls back two unsteady steps. He shoots me a look that says: "You were right."

Dad taps my arm and says, "Kally, let's bring the tools up from the beach." He stands up from the table. I gather up the paint and brush that Ollie brought me.

When we reach the beach steps, I can't not look back. Jennifer's face has sunk with worry. Mark is gesturing apologetically. Stuart has gone rigid, arms folded across his chest as if he is holding himself back from breaking into a run.

I turn away. It *is* a small island. And it's getting smaller.

As I follow Dad down the stairs to the beach, it's hard to understand what I'm seeing on the sand below us. The ocean rowboat sports a stubby mast that Dad fashioned out of what was left of *Home*'s. Luffing in the breeze is an undersized but good enough sail that he has sewn together from the scraps that had beached alongside *Home*. And, by the looks of his worksite, he is all set to rig the rudder.

Home lives on in the highly irregular form of this mongrel craft.

Dad and I quietly set to completing the transformation. Above a dent in the aluminum stern, I take my time painting the name we chose: *Home 2.0*. Half an hour later, I take a step back from our rejig and pronounce: "She's a scrappy-looking mutt."

Dad smiles for the first time since we got here. I take a seat on a jumble of driftwood and watch him make final adjustments to the pieced-together rudder.

"Stuart told me he wants to be a Flight Controller for NASA—or nothing," I say, curious about how the Hart family meeting is going topside.

"Let's hope he gets to do that," Dad says. But he has lost his smile, and there's no hope to be heard in his voice.

For weeks, walls of denial have been separating me and Dad from what is most real—and from each other. Today, we knocked a few chinks in them. On impulse, I take a sledge hammer to what is left.

"When I went to orientation for next week's college tours, it was hard enough being the strange new transfer student from the big city. And then, I find out their school theme for last year was 'Dream Your Future.' Everybody must have done their homework, because on the sign-up sheet for the tours, I was the only one who didn't fill in the blank next to: 'My Dream.' So, yeah, why didn't you and Mom ever convene a family meeting about—you know— my dreams for my future? You called meetings for everything else. Why not that?"

Dad gives up on his efforts to balance *Home 2.0*'s unorthodox rudder and glowers at her picked-over remains. I can't tell if he is coming to grips with how to answer my question—or avoiding it altogether. But you know what? Even if *no one* can answer them, evading the real questions is no longer an option. That ruinous strategy went out with Life, BEC.

So, I try again. "If we had talked about, you know, *the future*, maybe I wouldn't be the only one on that college tour who *isn't* obsessing over my college plans, sharing my major on Facebook, ticking off life goals in my life planner, gushing about how I cannot wait to visit that interdisciplinary program about—"

"Yeah, maybe."

"Maybe what?"

"Maybe we should have talked about your future, that's all."

"Why *maybe?*" I demand, dredging up my last shreds of patience. I stand up and try to pace off the tension. I can't believe he is still making me decode what he's saying and guess what he's not.

Then, suddenly, I get it. And the energy I've been running on these last two days from I don't know where drains out of my body, into the sand.

"Oh, right, of course." I droop down and sit on a piece of driftwood. "Why would my parents want to help me imagine my future? That would be the cruelest joke you could play on your kid. The future is *already here*. And guess what? It's nothing but wall-to-wall upheaval. Any dream I *would* have had is already meaningless."

Dad looks genuinely spooked. He sets the rudder down on the sand.

"Kally, no, you've got it all wrong. The things that need doing now, they're not meaningless. They're more vital than ever."

"If I'm so wrong, why do I feel like something died? Not just the future I could have had—but the whole future, the future itself. You know, with a capital 'F.'"

"Kally, that's not—"

"All the same, I still want to know what my dream *would* have been." I scoop a handful of sand and let it spill through my fingers. "Even if its expiration date just ran out."

Standing up from his seat on *Home*, Dad stumbles and catches himself. "Hearing you say what you just said—that is exactly what your mother and I knew we couldn't bear to hear from our—"

"Well, we're all going to have to bear lots of things we didn't think we could, aren't we?"

My eyes burn with the heat of tears. "I'm going up," I say.

Halfway up the beach stairs, I hear Dad call out, "Kally,

wait."

I stop and look back at him. "I *have* waited—to say what I just said—and to hear what I just heard." My panoramic view of ocean, wrecked pier, and *Home*'s pillaged body compels me to add, "There is nothing else to wait for—it's already here, remember?"

Dad looks desperate. Which is heart-wrenching. If only this could be one of those routine disaster simulations that he used to lead people in.

I drag myself back onto the one plan I've got for my so-called future and say, "I don't care if the Harts are done with their family meeting or not. I am going to finish fixing that satellite dish. Finding Mom. That is the only thing that matters now."

As I top the beach steps, I spot Stuart kicking storm debris away from the lighthouse door. The vibes coming off of him are urgent. Defiant. He yanks open the door and disappears inside.

That looked like a guy who wants to be left alone. I bet I looked the same way when Stuart found me sulking on the beach. He made me talk to him, anyway.

I'm glad that he did.

DREAMS

 on the spiral of tower stairs, I lean through the shattered window that overlooks the beach—and Dad. He might seem to be occupied with attaching *Home 2.0*'s patched-up rudder, but I recognize that Dad behavior. He's doing a whole-body think-through of what we just said to each other.

As I climb higher, broken glass crunches under my shoes and clinks down the metal steps. Holes gape where thick, wavy panes of glass used to be, framing the views in a seagull's perspective. It is stunningly gorgeous out there—if you don't dwell on the broken objects that St. Elmo's Whirlwind blew across the grounds.

Above my head, through the top deck's iron grate floor, I can see Stuart pacing laps around the lighthouse lantern. I decide it's only right to request permission to come aboard.

"Is it OK if I—?"

"Whatever."

I climb the last of the stairs and sit on the top one, so as not to obstruct Stuart's lap lane. The next time he circles past, I steal a glance at his face, trying to decide whether I should say something or respect his steely silence. On lap three, he solves my problem.

"That look you saw them giving each other?" he says. "I've been seeing it too. For days." He pulls off his NASA cap and rubs his hand over his head. "I thought they were upset because I was leaving home for the school year. Turns out, it's because they knew I *wasn't*."

His voice echoes in the tower for the time it takes him to complete another circuit around the lantern. He slaps his cap against his leg to the beat of his steps, and on the next pass, the furrow above his eyes cuts deeper.

"My dad consults for NASA a couple times a year. Two weeks ago—*two weeks*—his friend there gave him a heads-up. He told my dad they were going to shut down the whole program."

"Your internship program?"

"No. NASA. The guy told Dad the White House decided to decommission the entire agency. He said the government needs NASA money for 'urgent national problems.'"

"Like *what?*" I ask, with righteous indignation, then promptly kick myself for posing such an irrelevant question when, really, I should be acknowledging what he is going through.

"Like what?" he asks. "Like, the entire country is running out of drinkable water, for one thing."

"Yeah, of course."

"Dad said NASA is supposed to pronounce itself dead sometime this week." Stuart stops in mid-lap on the far side of the lantern. Framed in its huge lens, his edges ripple with rainbow colors.

"My parents thought I should hear it from them first. Out here." He forces a laugh and slaps his hat against the railing. "They thought all I needed was a week of deserted island living to decide what to do now. Like, there's a grab bag filled with lives and all I need to do is reach in and pull out a new one. Like, the life that just got scrubbed isn't the only one I'd ever want."

My first impression of Stuart might have dubbed him a cocky suburban jock who gets everything he wants. But that wasn't the whole story then, and for sure, it isn't now. I take another stab at offering some comfort.

"I thought you were so lucky because you knew what you wanted to do with your life," I say. "But now, I'm not so sure."

"Yeah?" His eyes are locked on the horizon, unseeing.

"Yeah. Maybe *I'm* the lucky one. I never had a dream to lose."

Stuart circles the deck again, then declares, "It's *not* lost!" He jams the NASA cap back on his head. "My dad's friend could be wrong. This could be a temporary setback. NASA's had plenty of them. Besides, it's too big to fail. With all that space junk up there, they'll need space garbage men if nothing else!" He stops pacing and grips the railing. "It's not lost."

For a second, I believe him—until his shoulders drop.

"How could you tell?" I ask. "You know, that being an astronaut was it?"

I'm surprised to hear the ache in my voice. He must hear it too, because his tone softens.

"Not an astronaut. A flight controller."

"Right, sorry, flight controller."

"I always knew."

Now the ache is in *his* voice.

"I wish I had always known, even if that meant I would have to change it now that everything is—" I still don't know how to finish that sentence.

Stuart comes around from behind the lantern and sits beside me on the step.

"You mean, you didn't always know you were going to be an anarchist? Or wait, was that—a *survivalist?*"

Part of me knows he is only trying to lighten the dreadful mood. But other parts are still super-sensitive when it comes to the topic of what I'm going to be when I grow up.

I lean away from him and declare, "Do you realize how gross it is to eavesdrop on other people's conversations when they are shipwrecked and trying really hard to—"

"Sorry," he says, but he does not look sorry. He looks like he is enjoying this. "I happened to be running on the bluff when you and your dad were talking on the beach. It's a—"

—we say it together—

"—small island."

I glare at him. That was neither amusing nor apologetic. Which, in my estimation, makes it my turn to step up to the watch deck and commence circling the lighthouse lantern, Stuart style.

"Do you know what next Monday is?" I don't wait for him to guess. "It's the day I'm supposed to get on a bus bound for five days of official college tours. And I haven't signed up for a single tour topic, because—what would I tour? I don't have a clue why I would even go to college. You want clues that rogue waves are coming? Whirlwinds are appearing on the horizon? And—yeah—force fields are barreling their way to your island? I've got them. But when it comes to what's coming in my life, all I have are blind spots. I had no clue my parents moved us to the Northwoods because they think it's the end of the world. No clue they've both been walking around fully aware that *it's already here*. And at this very moment, I have no clue if they're breaking up or just taking a break."

I'm not finished. I'm catching my breath.

"*No clue* that I would be living out of my backpack on the kindness of strangers. Unable to text my friends from my old school because my phone got drowned. Not knowing if my mom is OK or not. Sucker-punched by the news that if she *really is* OK, she is holed up somewhere that is semi-safe with a collective of artists who are protesting— everything, most likely—in the throes of what could be the last days of New York City. Hell, it could be the last days of the whole continent by now, because—yeah—that is actually the kind of thing I *do* get clues about. And from the looks of the demented scratchings in my sketchbook, I'd say there is a real good chance that these *are* the last days of—"

As I orbit past him, Stuart reaches out and catches my arm. "Whoa, time for reentry," he says, and swings me onto the stair beside him. As I catch my breath, he says, "Look, Kally, we're cut off from everything. Without reliable data, what's been happening these past couple of days seems like a disaster when maybe it's just a temporary setback. Trying to make decisions from out here is like freerunning with your hat pulled over your eyes. So, priority number one is to get off this island and go see for ourselves what's going on."

"And then?"

"Then, we'll adjust for it."

I inspect the lighthouse grounds through the cracked window at my shoulder. It *is* hard to tell if I'm viewing a disaster or something we can adjust for. But as I add up what we *do* know is going on, even from here, plus all the stuff we *don't* know—

"I want to believe you." I fight the quavering in my voice. "I want to believe we can adjust for all this. But I can't unsee what is in my drawings."

I'm inches away from Stuart's eyes, and what I see in *them* is—how totally real he is being with me. Which is why I let myself say, "My drawings say that minor adjustments are not enough, Stuart. They say we have to re-rig our entire lives, fore to aft, if we want to go on living at all."

The way Stuart stares at me, I get the feeling he's looking right through me at a chasm he doesn't know how to leap, because nobody does. And it's coming up on us, fast. It's what we've been trying to tune out but can't, no matter how distracted we try to make ourselves. But the thing I've started to realize about Stuart is—when a chasm opens up at his feet, he doesn't stall out. He detects whatever forward momentum there is to be had—and he hitches a ride on it.

"Come on," Stuart says, jumping up. He takes my hand and urges me down the spiral with him. "We'll get that satellite dish working. Then, I'll ask my dad to call the guy with the only boat that's still working and tell him to come and get us. You'll email your mom and find out where she is—so we can figure out how to bring her home. I bet as soon as your family is back together—your drawings will give you all sorts of clues about your future."

"What about yours?" Our voices echo dizzily around the whitewashed walls of the tower as I lurch, Stuart gazelles, down the stairs.

"NASA is too big to fail. I'll work for whatever is left of it," he says. "My future is A-OK."

It feels good to see Stuart back in that freerunner zone of his. All it took was one long, tense dinner discussion dedicated to convincing his parents that NASA is sure to endure in one form or another. And that whatever it turns into, it is bound to need an intern. In the end, Jennifer and Mark agreed that the minute they are off this island, they will drive with him to Houston and make sure he is first in line.

But before anything even close to that can happen, we must get our now-working satellite dish talking to a still-functioning satellite. Which is why, at this moment, Stuart is straddling the rooftop of the shack and aiming the dish at pinpoints of light.

I fidget at the foot of the creaky wooden ladder, Stuart's phone gripped in my hand, eyes locked on the screen. One bar lights up.

"Wait, go back," I call up to the roof.

Stuart swivels the dish a few inches eastward.

"Stop! OK, three bars!" I report.

"Check your email before it drops," Stuart shouts from the roof.

"I'm trying, but it's so slow. Uh! No! Zero bars again."

Jennifer walks up. "Stuart? Can you even see what you're doing up there?" She pulls the blanket tighter around her sweater. "It's late. You two should get some sleep."

"We'll sleep after we get emails off to the keeper and Kally's mom."

"I hope you reach her soon," Jennifer says to me.

This is the least nervous I've seen Stuart's mom since we shipwrecked. I can imagine how relieved she is that there's one less family secret to keep, and—yeah—that her son is still talking to her after its disclosure.

"Is my dad—?"

"Out cold on the couch," Mark says, appearing out of the darkness.

I nod.

He hands me a laptop, and says, "When you find a satellite signal, connect the dish directly into this. That will be more stable than if you go through the WiFi. And it's easier to type on than a phone."

Jennifer's eyes narrow. "You said you wouldn't bring a computer. You promised."

"It's the old one from the office," Mark says, as if that made it not count as a computer.

Finally, we are locked on to a steady satellite signal. But the same message has been glowing on the screen for hours: "You Are Not Connected to the Internet."

Stuart and I hunch over his dad's laptop at a small table in the corner of the shack. We pulled the blankets off of Stuart's cot and we're wearing them like superhero capes.

Our powers are hardly super. Servers must be down

worldwide. If the message ever changes to "connected," I have a cramped finger poised above "get mail."

Ollie comes in from outside, moving like one of the living dead, her bedspread wound tightly around her.

"You guys, why are you up?" she yawns.

"Uh huh," Stuart says, staring at the screen.

Eyes half closed, Ollie shuffles up to the bench of monitors that are connected to the weather instruments outside. With their chunky black dials, green screens etched with graphs, and fat wires going everywhere, they would make perfect props for a 1950s sci-fi movie.

Watching Ollie, even in her sleepwalking state, it's easy to guess what her dream future is. She must think it just came true as she spins the monitors' dials and blinks at their flickering amber lights.

She ambles over to the ham radio and clicks its tarnished copper Morse Code key a few times.

"Help me fix our weather station tomorrow, OK Stuart?"

"Uh huh."

"I could be missing something really big." Ollie wipes cobwebs off the window above the radio. "Is the internet on yet?" She plops into the operator's chair.

"On and off," I say, rubbing my eyes.

"Mostly off." Stuart says.

Ollie stands back up and waddles across the room to our table.

"I gotta check the weather news when the internet turns back on."

"After Kally sends her email," Stuart says. Suddenly, he snaps to attention. "Try now!" he says.

My finger stabs the "get mail" key. The rainbow spins a few times and then, in the list of unread mail, in bold, the name "Tracy Guthrie" appears.

I grab Stuart's arm.

"That's her, that's my mom."

"Come on, load," Stuart coaxes the screen.

I hold my breath as the laptop chugs.

"There!" I shout. "It's from yesterday!" I speed read Mom's words and squeeze Stuart's arm again. "She's OK. She says she's OK."

Stuart stretches in his chair and smiles.

"Awesome!" Ollie cheers.

"She's worried because she knows we went sailing. She's trying to get home. But she says it's impossible to travel. The cell towers don't work. Only a few blocks of the city have electricity. 'Please keep trying to reach me. Tell me that you're OK. I'll keep trying to—'"

I scroll down. But there is nothing more to read. I start hitting "get mail" over and over.

"She could have lost the signal," Stuart says.

Right then, our laptop's satellite connection drops from four bars to one, to zero.

"No!" I hit the desk with my fist. Mom was here with me. She was here in this room! Now she is—I don't know where.

"Draft your email back to her," Stuart says. "The second even one bar shows up, hit 'send.'"

I pound out a reply to my mom's cut-off message. I tell her where we are, that we are OK, that she has got to keep trying to send messages to us, no matter what.

We sit and stare at the line of flat internet bars. My finger shakes above the "send" key.

"When she gets my message and hears we're not at home, she'll be even more worried," I say.

We wait.

"There's so much I want to tell her," I say.

"The signal is back!" Stuart says.

My finger jabs "send." A label appears: "sent." I wish I could believe it.

"We should check the news before the connection drops again," Stuart says.

While I bring up news sites on Mark's laptop, Stuart connects his phone to the WiFi, and his thumbs fly. Before long, he's muttering "holy shit" over and over.

"What!?" Ollie asks, each time he does.

"Just keep reading, everything you can," I tell Stuart.

"Come on you guys. What's happening?" Ollie implores.

"We'll tell you in a minute, Ollie," Stuart says.

I sense a shift in Stuart's energy. He's staring at his phone. But he's not reading the screen.

"Stuart?" I reach to touch his arm.

His phone slides out of his hand and drops into Ollie's. He backs away from us, turning left, then right. "I—I'm— I've got to go for a run," he says.

"But it's night," Ollie calls after him.

The radio shack door bangs shut behind him.

I take Stuart's phone from Ollie and read the blunt headline aloud: "President Disbands NASA."

I put my arm around Ollie's shoulders, and we walk to the door. When our eyes adjust to the blackness, we see Stuart break into a freerunning leap aimed at the railing that encircles the lighthouse. But his feet skid crazily along it and he crash-lands to the ground.

He rises halfway to his knees, then sits back down. He puts his head in his hands. His shoulders shake.

Ollie sinks to the floor and sits cross-legged in the doorway. As she watches over her brother, I smooth her hair.

After a few minutes, I set out across the grounds and sit on the grass behind Stuart. I give him plenty of space. But I know he can tell that I am here.

And this is how Day One, AEC ends. Me, sitting in the dark under the twirling lighthouse beam, tending Stuart's silhouette, while surreal headlines replay in my mind.

From what I could tell, in the past 48 hours, dreaded tipping points rammed into dreaded tipping points and compounded. Failing planetary systems spawned scores of freakish, cataclysmic events around the entire globe. As of tonight, human life on Earth has tipped into—yeah—seriously changed. The things that happened to us, from the rogue wave to St. Elmo's Whirlwind, wouldn't be worth a mention in the news I just read. What happened here were minor, local ripples.

Slowly, Stuart's silhouette goes from broken and bent to just plain spent. It stirs. His back straightens. His shoulders reset. His spirit must be gathering itself up again.

That's good. We will need all the spirit we can summon. One soul-shaker of a future has arrived, and—yeah—it's ours.

DAY TWO, AEC

 the walls at opposite sides of the kitchen, cradling their respective coffee mugs.

Mark is at the table, chin propped on his fist, poking a screwdriver at the guts of the AM radio that he has been trying to fix forever.

Ollie frowns on her cereal, which is only semi-moist now that Jennifer has imposed milk rationing.

Stuart and I are stationed just inside the door where a slash of morning sun blazes through the screen and warms my toes. We've come from our all-nighter at the laptop. When a functioning satellite flew over and the internet decided to work, whoever was the most awake grabbed fragments of news from the outside world. Now, we are here to deliver the morning edition of the news.

"We emailed the keeper and told him we would pay the guy with the boat to come right now and take us back,"

Stuart says. "But we're not sure it actually went. Anyway, there's no reply yet."

"Mom didn't get any of our emails," I report. "She still doesn't know where we are. But the message that came at 2 a.m. said she's still fine, even though the city isn't. The people she's with are being brave and calm, but nothing is working and there's hardly any food left. She sent the address where she's helping out at an emergency center. It's in the Bowery. She's trying to find a way out of the city so she can come home. She says we'll have so many stories to tell each other. And that she loves us. Both."

Dad doesn't say anything. He steps to the window above the sink and surveys the sunrise.

Stuart takes it from there. "They shut down nuclear power plants in seven states because of region-wide flooding. They say blackouts and brownouts are happening everywhere east of the Mississippi. It must be true, because as soon as an email server comes online, the internet signal to our dish drops. And when our dish finds a working satellite again, it's the email servers that are out."

"The last time we downloaded news was 3:00 a.m.," I say. Then I notice that I'm starving and head for the kitchen table. "Mom had to write a few sentences and hit send before she lost her connection." I give the three cereal boxes on the table a dull look. "Her email was like a string of one-line telegrams."

"Which is smart—given the rolling power failures," Stuart says. "The grid's not a grid anymore, just a mess of surges and blown transformers. Everyone is making it worse by trying to get information and check on each other. As of this morning, the news sites reverted to text-only mode. It's like the old internet—or the first moon shot."

"The power grid in the eastern half of the country is outdated," Dad says from his lookout at the window. "They have known for years that if something big stressed it—solar flare, cyber-attack, heat waves—the surges would blow transformers the length of the East Coast and deep into the Midwest. They don't have enough spare parts to repair or replace even a small fraction of those transformers."

"But that is just plain stupid," Jennifer sputters. "Why didn't they take care of that?

Everyone gives her their personal version of the look that says: "you're really asking that?"

Stuart takes a deep breath and pulls himself up to his full height. "And, it's official. They dissolved NASA. The whole thing."

Jennifer hurries across the kitchen and reaches to touch his arm. "Oh. Stuart." She turns to Mark. "It's happening so fast."

Mark hauls himself off the kitchen chair and picks up the battered radio. He carries it across the room to Stuart and looks his son in the eyes. "We'll do our best," Mark says.

Stuart nods and takes the radio. He turns it over in his hands a few times, then walks it to the electric outlet beside the frig and plugs it in. The backup generator behind the shack growls like it lost a muffler. The radio crackles and zaps sparks.

"That smells bad," Ollie says.

Stuart yanks the plug out of the socket.

"Now it's dead," Ollie groans.

At that, Dad finally turns from the window and activates his emergency manager voice. "We need to know how long we will be out here. We need information."

"There's that vintage ham station in the shack," Stuart says, laying the radio's smoking skeleton on the kitchen table.

"It can't do voices, I checked," Ollie says. "It only does Morse Code. We don't learn that at camp 'till next summer."

"They must have a book on that around here somewhere," I say through a mouthful of sticky dry cereal that I randomly selected and am eating straight from the box.

"I can do it." Jennifer waves her coffee cup casually in the air.

"Do what?" Mark asks.

"Morse Code."

"You can?" Ollie's eyes grow big.

"I learned it in college." Jennifer downs the rest of her coffee.

Stuart looks at his mom like he just met her. "Why did you learn *that?*"

"I had to if I wanted to make the team."

"What team?" Mark asks, his eyes as wide as Ollie's.

"The one that played in the first cellphone-based urban game ever," Jennifer says. "Which, we won."

Her family continues to stare at Jennifer as if she's a marvel. But Dad fully recognizes her as someone who just held out a straw, and he reaches for it.

"We need an estimate on how long we'll be stranded here," Dad says. "Can you can get the Coast Guard on that ham radio?"

Jennifer stiffens and squeezes the coffee cup with both hands. "It was so long ago. It was a game. On cellphones. I never sent code on a real radio—only on a flip phone."

"I'll help!" Ollie says, latching on to her mom's elbow and pulling her toward the door.

The generator labors outside the shack. Inside, Jennifer sits at attention in front of the ham radio. Its dials are glowing, but the only sound coming from it is the electric hum of its own innards.

Ollie watches, entranced, as her mother recites the alphabet and taps Morse Code on the wooden bench with her fingernails. Which, I can't help noticing, are painted moody metallic.

As I duck under the bench and fish in the toolbox for wire cutters, I hear Jennifer mumbling to herself, "What's 'W' again?"

Back outside, I head up the ladder and deliver the cutters to the roof. Stuart is up there once again, sitting astride the peak, horseback rider style.

Balancing myself on the third rung from the top, I hold antenna wires steady as Stuart trims their storm-ripped ends. He twists them together to reconnect the kinked-in antenna tower in front of us to the ham radio inside the shack. I use the tip of the cutters to give the connection an extra turn for good measure.

We hold our breaths. Our eyebrows are raised.

A second later, Morse Code blasts from inside the shack.

Jennifer finishes drafting her message in large dots and dashes and lays her cheat sheet on the bench in front of her.

For the next hour, she alternates between pecking out our call for help, and struggling to make sense of the insanely fast stream of long and short tones that crackle in and out of the static.

All of us have been hanging out in the shack as if combining our nervous energy will boost Jennifer's efforts. And maybe it does, because out of nowhere, someone answers her. Turns out, nowhere is in Newfoundland.

"Why was she talking to Canada?" Ollie asks, utterly confused.

"Because somebody up there finally slowed down enough to listen to your mom," Mark says. "She asked them to relay her call to the East Ledge Coast Guard, and they did. So, now she is finished with talking to Canada, and she's talking straight to the Coast Guard."

"Oh." Ollie brightens.

"S l o w e r." Jennifer mutters the word as she keys it haltingly. The incoming code decelerates. She seizes a pencil and scribbles strings of dots and dashes. Above them, she fills in the letters that she's able to remember.

"I think they're asking how much food we have. I'll say, 'enough for a week.'" She works the key at a slow crawl.

After a full minute of excruciating radio silence, a series of scratchy tones comes back. We lean in closer and watch Jennifer spell the message on her notepad: "s i t t i g h t"

"That's it? 'Sit tight?'" Stuart is incredulous.

The mood of the adults in the room swings from buoyant to flatlined.

Ollie, on the other hand, is jubilant. "Awesome!" she says. "We get to stay! I'm gonna go fix our weather instruments." She streaks out the door.

"Ask them how long we're supposed to 'sit tight,'" Stuart says.

"They signed off." Jennifer exhales and pitches back in her chair.

I selfishly ignore Jennifer's frazzled state and clutch the arm of her chair seat.

"Please, call them back," I plead. "They have to find Mom and let her know we're here. They have got to help her get home."

"Of course, Kally," Jennifer says. "If they're too busy, I guess I could try to find that ham operator in Canada again. He could pass your message to someone in the city, and maybe whoever gets it there could—"

But, before she can finish, the walls and contents of the building, our bodies included, recoil under booming reverberations.

Fingers in her ears and squealing, Ollie bursts into the shack—startled and delighted at the same time.

The foghorn atop our lighthouse has bellowed to life.

Minutes later, we are lined up along the rim of the bluff, hands covering our ears. A grim beast of a fog bank surges toward us out of the otherwise cloudless morning. As it advances on our island, the temperature plummets and the atmosphere turns heavy with water gone airborne.

I huddle against Dad and watch a lowering cloud the color of steel wool slink along the surface of the ocean. It obliterates the sandbar, sweeps the beach, then levitates up the side of the sand cliff.

Ollie shrieks and shrinks away from the ragged gray

tendrils as they crest the dune and slither past us. When they close ranks behind our backs, their cold droplets attach to our skin and clothes. We are covered in millions of translucent beads of mist.

The roiling mass presses on and thickens, erasing all signs of the lighthouse, radio shack, and finally, even the keeper's house.

The ground clouds arrived hours ago, and the internet has been down ever since. Stuart finally gave up his satellite signal stakeout and announced that if he didn't go for a freerun, he would cease functioning altogether. He is out there now, inching his way to the beach.

I've been lending moral support to Jennifer from my seat on Stuart's cot. Every time the foghorn thunders, she loses a chunk of code. Thanks to the all-nighter news watch Stuart and I pulled, I keep nodding off even as I fight to maintain an upright position.

Finally, we admit to each other that Dad's assessment must be right. Due to what the news sites said was happening, and now this blackout fog, we East Ledge Islanders have sunk to the bottom of the Coast Guard's priority list.

At first, Jennifer's strategy was to raise East Ledge's Coast Guard again so she could tell them about my mom. When that failed, she changed tack and started begging ham operators to slow down and answer her plea for a message relay to New York City.

I keep trying to convince her that it's OK to take a break. But she promised me she would do everything she could to reach my mom, and she is taking it as a sacred obligation to motherhood.

When she finally tears herself from the radio, she stretches, shuffles over to Stuart's cot, and collapses into sleep.

I exit the shack as quietly as possible. In the wet murk, I have to search for the path to the keeper's house. Setting out along it, I savor the thought that near total darkness at midday as the perfect occasion for chipping away at my own sleep deprivation.

I was so wrong.

I bang various body parts against the paneling of the bunk cave in futile efforts to fashion ear muffs out of pillow and blanket. I sit up and stuff more toilet paper in my ears. I speculate as to how many lighthouse keepers went raving mad from being blasted and vibrated inside the force fields of their foghorns. I give up.

I reach for a pen and open my sketchbook to a new page. But the fog outside the house has got nothing on the fog inside my brain.

I stare at the blank page until, at last, exhaustion trumps foghorn.

FALLING AND LANDING

 of consciousness, I force my eyes open to—total darkness. Unable to see my own pillow, I conclude that the fog has gone preternatural and achieved a state of 100% opaqueness. The rising wave of panic subsides only when I come to realize that the reason there is no sunlight is because—yeah—it's night. I have been out for over twelve hours.

Wide awake on adrenalin, I pull wads of tissue paper out of my ears and listen for signs of life between foghorn bellows. Someone tosses in their bed upstairs. Ollie calls out weakly, "When is it going to stop?" I can't tell if she is awake or dreaming. It's too dark to see into the sitting room, but I suspect the snoring that is going in and out of sync with the foghorn is Dad's.

My sleeping nook isn't merely lightless, it is cramped, damp, and claustrophobic. I lower myself out of the bunk, grope my way to the door, and peer into the fog-clenched hours between Day Two and Day Three, AEC. The darkness pulsates with horn blasts. Overhead, suspended water droplets burst into billions of swirling points of light with each sweep of the lighthouse beam.

Ever since the rogue wave put its kink in reality, time has passed in jerks and stutters. And now, this hovering density has smothered any sense of it.

If I ignore all the events on yesterday's inventory list of AEC insanities, I guess I could say that in a highly roundabout way, I'm getting what I hoped to get this weekend. No internet, no smart phone, no texts messages, no college course catalogues, no peer pressure to know what I am supposed to be making of my life. Which means, there is nothing to jam whatever signals I could be picking up about what is on its way—for *me*.

The trouble is, being out here with no distractions is making what is happening for everyone else—everywhere else—feel *closer than ever*. I'm picking up signals about "what's on its way for me" all right. They are loud and clear. *All of this* is on its way for me. Because it is on its way for everyone.

I've been half aware of a faint glow appearing and disappearing between the billowing curtains of gloom outside the door. When the glow returns, I decide it must be from the radio shack's window. Stuart can't sleep either.

I could follow the light through the fog to the shack. I could see if Stuart wants to talk about—anything. If I do, it will change things. It usually does when you ask someone if they would like to talk, just talk, about—nothing in particular. Stuart and I might go from being randomly thrown together castaways to…friends. Having Stuart for a friend would change lots of things. Stuart…a fellow traveler…in all this weirdness.

Fog roils around my head as I stand at the open door of the radio shack, sketchbook clutched in my hand. "I think it's getting to me," I say.

"It's just as loud in here, but there's less fog," Stuart replies.

I take that to be an invitation.

One foot barely makes it into the shack and I'm spilling a nervous rush of words. "The foghorn has a strange echo, don't you think? It sounds like it's bouncing off of something. Out that way." I point my sketchbook vaguely in the direction of the ocean. "I couldn't say how an echo acts in a fog like this. I have never seen fog like this. Have you? I wouldn't be surprised if this fog was thick enough to behave like a solid wall and bounce foghorn echoes!"

I couldn't sound more off-kilter, or more echo science geeky.

"Can't say I noticed." Stuart pulls the blanket off his cot and places it around my shoulders.

I'm surprised at how clumsily he did that, and even more surprised at how shy it's made me. "Oh, thanks," I say.

Stuart takes an awkward step back. "Maybe it's bouncing off the water's surface. The foghorn, I mean." He steers himself to the pile of boxes he has stacked on the floor.

"Um, it *is* bouncing off the ocean. All foghorns do that. But, um, there's a second echo—coming from farther out." I stuff my sketchbook into my hoodie pocket, pull Stuart's blanket tighter around myself, and scan the room for anything to change the subject.

"So. You're still doing inventory. My dad was too, before the 100% humidity drove him into a fetal position on the couch."

"If 'sit tight' is Coast Guard for 'more than a week,' we'll be needing things. That door leads to a storeroom," he says, pointing to the far wall. "I found a crate of window panes in there. We can use them to repair what broke. I was about to check out what's under the cot." He opens the flaps on a large cardboard box.

"I hope it's their stash of earplugs. What could be more essential to life on East Ledge?" I say.

He smiles, and I finally understand why I keep track of each time he does: Stuart smiles only when he means it.

"Sorry, no earplugs, just sheet metal." He holds up squares of tin. "For general repairs, probably. But, hey, I found one outstanding weather balloon!" He unzips the long duffle bag lying next to him on the floor.

"Weather balloon? Ollie will freak," I say, laughing.

I walk over to the bench to check on the laptop. "Any internet?"

"One bar shows up maybe once every hour. But it lasts only five or ten seconds."

I touch a key. Mark's laptop comes to life with its browser frozen on a pixilated news site. I close it and aim for the restart button—then pull back my hand. Hiding behind the browser was a video player, paused on a frame.

"Movies? You've been hoarding movies during this entertainment emergency?" I take a seat at the laptop and reach for the "play" button.

Stuart jumps away from the weather balloon. "That's just a video my dad had on his desktop." He leans past my shoulder to close the laptop. But before he can, I catch hold of the edge of the screen.

"Hey, it's you!" I say. In the freeze frame, I recognize Stuart, in a city, freerunning along a rooftop.

"Can I play it?"

Stuart scowls. I hold my sketchbook up to his eyes.

"You saw *this*. You owe me."

Stuart turns away and goes back to opening boxes.

I hit play. Whoever is working the camera is having a hard time keeping up with Stuart as he freeruns through streets and public squares. It reminds me of one of those leaping tiger flying dragon movies. I lean closer to the screen and try to detect the special effects. But there aren't any. What I'm watching is all Stuart.

"This is incredible. It looks like you're running along an invisible thread strung through the city. No—it's more like your feet are laying that thread down as you go."

Stuart comes up behind me to watch the video.

"Is freerunning part of your NASA training?" I ask.

"It might as well be. They both come down to the same things."

"And that would be?"

"Thinking on the fly. Quick work arounds. Navigating twists that you never expected." He turns his back on the screen and prods the limp weather balloon with his shoe. "Anyway, that's what I used to think," he says.

"As in—past tense," I say.

He picks up pieces of weather balloon gear, then sets them back down on the floor. "I've been playing that video all night. From here, everything about it seems…wrong. There is no way to work around what's going on now. We're facing nothing but obstacles in all directions. Obstacles with no handholds or footholds in sight."

He shoves a few pieces of balloon gear back into the bag, then walks to the screen door and glares out at the fog.

"Footholds and handholds," I say, turning the images over in my mind. "Maybe you're not supposed to be looking for them anymore."

"That foghorn really got to you," he says into the grayness that presses at the door.

"No, seriously, look at this." I rewind the video and hit "play." "You're watching for footholds and handholds every second, right? Which means, you're always zoomed in on *details*, like that little crack in the wall you just grabbed."

Oozing skepticism, Stuart rejoins me at the laptop. I replay the last few seconds of the video. Stuart hits pause and jabs a spot on the screen.

"See that 'little crack' in the wall?" he asks. "*That* is what kept me from falling two stories. I wouldn't call that a detail."

I'm sure the foghorn was shredding his patience before I got here. And now I'm daring to offer opinions on his masterful command of freerunning.

"Yes. No. But—" I stammer, then say, "Never mind. I am the last person who should be talking about finding footholds in life. Not to mention, I have zero knowledge about freerunning."

"Maybe so. But you knew about that rogue wave. And the whirlwind. So, you can't stop now. Come on, but what?"

"The thing is," I try again, "if you're looking only at the

details, at the surfaces of things, then sure, you can do some things really well. Like, winning freerunning championships."

"Yeah. You can. But?"

"But that means you're not looking at what is happening deeper, or farther away. You're not looking at the bigger picture."

"That's right. And you know why not?" Stuart drags the radio operator's chair next to mine and sits, facing me, elbows on knees. "Let's say, in the middle of a vault or halfway between Earth and Mars, you hit a snag that you didn't see coming. Let's say it trips you up big time. Now, you're forced to come up with a fix on the fly. If you want even the slightest chance of doing that, you better be wide awake and, damn right, you better be focused on what's smack in front of your face."

He turns to the screen, rewinds the video, and hits "pause."

"See that ledge?" he asks, pointing to a window in what looks like a warehouse. "It has a slight tilt. At this precise point in the run, that little surface detail is the most critical fact of all. The ledge is tilted *up*, not down. If I'm alert enough to note that detail in time, I can land my fingertips here, and turn that tilt into a handhold. But, if I'm thinking about some 'bigger picture' instead, I miss that opportunity. And my head smashes open. See what I'm saying? It's simply not practical to be looking at whatever the bigger picture is that you're talking about."

"Uh-huh."

"What."

"Nothing." I stare at the cover of my sketchbook.

Stuart leans back in his chair and shakes his head. "If you're seeing something in that video that I need to know about, you've got to say so. We're talking matters of life and death here."

We *are* talking matters of life and death. I stand and step away from the table. "Fine, here's what I have to say: *Really?* You really don't see what is going on under all these surfaces that you've been freerunning on?"

But no, by the searching look on his face, I can tell he's not seeing what I'm seeing.

"OK, listen." I try to calm myself by pacing in front of Stuart's chair. "Isn't what we have been calling 'civilization' smashing its head against one big-ass wall that we all should have seen coming? And isn't that because we humans have been paying attention to *nothing but* what's in front of our own personal faces? Aren't we collectively cracking our heads into all sorts of obstacles that we have created for ourselves because we weren't paying attention to—yeah— the bigger picture?"

That sounded like my mother. But who cares? It's what I believe. So, I continue.

"Most of what makes up life on this planet *never* shows up on the surface. It's working at way deeper levels. And it's in the threads that connect all the levels to each other. Those *connections* are what keep things, you know, *going*—as in, living and breathing. Some of the most 'matter of life and death' stuff there is will never get up in your face. But that doesn't mean you can just act like it's not there. Up here on the surface of things, humans are chasing their dream futures, steamrolling across the planet, treating it as if it's a black-topped parking lot. But it's not a parking lot. It's a network of vital connections from the surface, all the way down."

Now I'm storming along the musty perimeter of the radio room, and when I come to the screen door, I gulp in waterlogged air and carry on. After all, these are matters of life and death.

"We broke your freerunner's code a million times over, Stuart. We haven't been *interacting* with the obstacles we meet. We have been slicing and dicing our ways through them, severing the threads that hold this whole blue marble show together. And—yeah—how well is *that* working for pretty much every last living thing? How *practical* is *that*?"

I sputter to a stop and slump into the nearest chair because I have run out of wind.

Behind me, and through the pounding in my ears, I hear Stuart's softened voice say, "It's about as practical as ignoring what is right here looking at you."

"Yeah? Like what?" I take more deep breaths.

When I turn to Stuart for an answer, his eyes look into mine. And right then, in my imagination, he says, "Like *me*."

In real life, however, I hear him saying, "Like these *pictures* you draw, that's what." He reaches for my sketchbook, which I've been waving around to emphasize my points, and holds it up to my eyes.

"You've been paying so much attention to those subsurface worlds of yours, you can't see what you have here."

He flips through the book and pronounces, "These lines you draw? They are the bleeding edges of brand-new facts of life on Earth."

I look at the drawing Stuart is displaying and try to decide if I have been flattered or incriminated. He can see there is need for further explanation.

"Kally, you've been drawing the fingertips of new realities. They're finding handholds and they are hauling themselves up into this world this very instant. You're picking up signals from what is so new and raw—it doesn't look like *anything* yet."

"Yeah, that's the problem exactly," I shoot back, taking the sketchbook from his hand. "What I draw doesn't look like *anything*. I used to believe these scribbled lines could be something important, something worth making, like my mom's art is. But you nailed it. Half-baked, looking like nothing—that's what my drawings are."

"That is not what I meant," Stuart says.

"Whatever, I've stopped making them." I toss the book onto the table.

"You can't stop," Stuart says. "These are signals from what's coming to the surface all around us. People need to see them." He picks up the sketchbook and pushes it into my hands.

"Own it, Kally. You're a human antenna."

For a minute there, I thought Stuart actually understood me. But then he had to say that last part. My embarrassed laughter alerts him to how much I am *not* sharing his enthusiasm for the prospect that—yeah—I'm a 'human antenna.' So, he pivots.

"Look, the signals are coming at you full force out here. It's too much to absorb. You need to tune out everything except the course you're running," he says.

I look down at the drawings on the open pages of my sketchbook. "But sometimes, the course is terrifying," I say.

"If you stand at the brink of a chasm and just stare at it, sure, that gets terrifying." Turning to the laptop, Stuart rewinds to one of his more harrowing leaps from rooftop to rooftop and plays it in slow motion. As I watch him launch into a slow-motion fall, my stomach drops—just like it did when *Home* topped a large wave.

"But," he says, "if you run toward the chasm with your entire self focused on calibration, adjustment, response— you cut off power to the part of you that is terrified. You redirect your energy to the part that is the running. When you do that, you stop seeing the chasm as a barrier of fear. You see it for what it *really* is."

"What is it, really?"

"Part of the course."

"The chasm is part of the course," I repeat. I have no idea what he is talking about, but this video isn't lying. I close my sketchbook and say, "Show me how you do that."

Tapping the pages of my sketchbook, Stuart says, "Sure, if you show me how you do *this.* "

Coming up with the challenges we just assigned ourselves was hard work, especially for the middle of the night. We were so caught up in the effort—we didn't notice that our foghorn had moaned its final moan. We even missed the silence that's been thundering in its wake. But, as we emerge from the shack, we are right on time to watch the midnight moon pierce through the last unraveling filaments of fog.

After so many hours of life in near darkness, our eyes strain to adjust to the lush moonlight. And when they do, there's plenty of light to work by.

Stuart takes 20 giant steps back from the brink of the sand cliff while I position myself at the base of the lighthouse. When Stuart turns to face the ocean, his focus is so concentrated, I can feel its force field from across the grounds. He is gathering his energy up and sending it deep into the ground all at the same time. Before I can even register the blastoff, he sprints past me and launches his entire self over the edge.

Stuart's transit through thin air lasts much longer than gravity should allow for anything that is not a bird. An impossible number of seconds later, he joins his feet with the sandy cliff-side and transmutes all of that flying energy into a graceful touch down. He throws in an effortless lope the rest of the way to the beach.

When he turns and looks up at me, his face beams in the moonlight.

"See what I mean?" he calls, bounding up the beach steps two at a time. "It's never just you. It's you plus wind, light, distances, temperatures, angles, velocity…"

"I'm not so sure. That looked like all you and nothing but you."

"It wasn't," he says, topping the steps and striding across the grounds. "That's why I'm able to do it at all."

He holds out his hand and I pass off my sketchbook for safekeeping.

Eyes fixed on the drop-off, I walk backwards a good 30 feet. I'm excited, but I'm scared, too. My spine stiffens and my body turns into dead weight.

"I'm not afraid of the falling part," I call out to him, and steal a few more steps back from the edge. "I'm afraid of the landing part. The crash-landing part."

"You can't have the falling without the landing," he calls back.

I won't argue with that.

"They're the same thing!" he shouts.

Now *that* I don't get. But I do remember Stuart saying something about how the chasm of fear I'm aimed at right now is part of the course. I try reciting in my head: *'Falling and landing, same thing. Chasms of fear, part of the course."* And suddenly, I notice that the moonlight has turned the space beyond the edge of the cliff into one continuous field of indigo.

The intensity of the roller coaster ride that we've been on these past two days has gotten coiled up—stuck—in my spine. My body senses its chance to let it all go, and without giving my head a say in the matter, it springs into a run.

As my arms and legs pump into a mad sprint, my mind begs them to remember something from that week in high school when we did gymnastics.

As my feet pound the last few yards of solid ground, in an act of sheer self-preservation, my body memory kicks in and executes its vague recollection of a regulation long jump. *Don't look down, jump up, shoot chest out, look to the sky, let arms lag…*

Momentum carries me impressively far beyond the cliff edge, and as it does, the wind around me takes on substance. I'm not falling through the atmosphere of our planet—I'm moving along its flowing forms. This must be how *Home* felt when she skimmed the sea's surface. And how Stuart feels when he freeruns rooftops. It's how my drawings feel when they…

Time's improbably long stretch snaps back to *now*! My

feet convert their fluid slide along the night air into a surprisingly gentle meet-up with the cliffside.

The landing.

In giant steps, I bound down the slope to the beach. I'm whooping with joy. I haven't whooped in weeks.

Stuart performs his second human glider feat of the night and joins me at water's edge.

Still catching my breath, I size up the cliff, unbelieving. When I look over at Stuart, it is with new levels of appreciation and curiosity. Who is this guy? How did he learn to move with the world this way? And—yeah—how does he know things about me and my drawings even *I* don't know?

Smiling, Stuart holds out my sketchbook.

"My turn," he says.

I used to think I saw tinges of smugness in these rare smiles of his. But it is ease and confidence that I've been seeing. And, I got something else wrong, too. Stuart is in touch with way more than what is right in front of him. He is every bit as tapped in as he thinks I am—in amazing, different ways.

I take my sketchbook from Stuart and welcome the challenge to chart a maiden voyage for him and *Home 2.0*.

Yesterday's storm rearranged our island's foreshore in major ways. Two hundred yards out to sea, we have gained an entirely new, sprawling sandbar, complete with surf foaming at its far edge.

Between the sandbar and beach, a pleasant tidal pool has formed. It is huge—at least several acres in size. The graceful curves of its boundaries are filling with the gentle, advancing waves of an incoming tide. The moon is high and the pool sparkles with its reflection.

The breeze that finally broke the grip of the dark-as-night fog is fresh, but not blustery.

In other words, a perfect time and place for a late-night sail.

I work the rudder while Stuart makes every effort to get the feel of *Home 2.0*'s makeshift boom. Each time the breeze oscillates, I have to improvise a new way to trim the seaweed-stained sail. That's because everything about *2.0* is wonky. How could it not be? But ten minutes into our shakedown cruise, I've gained a good enough sense of her highly non-regulation sail and rudder. Dad did an uncanny job of engineering her. Parts of *Home* are alive and well in this mongrel of a sailboat! I can feel it in the way she and the wind are flirting with each other.

Finally, we are as steady on the water as we're going to be. Time to teach Stuart how I come to draw the fingertips of new forces breaking into the world. Which is laughable, because I have no clue how what he sees in my sketchbook gets there. But I do know that some force fields are not mysterious at all. Even Stuart could tell when they're on their way.

I wait until we reach the far north end of the tidal pool, then coax *Home 2.0* to come about. As we head south on a port tack, we make such good headway, I actually forget for a second that we aren't in a real sailboat.

Let the lesson begin.

"Things that you *can* see and feel on the surface out here—you know, wind, waves, currents, temperatures—they're not even close to the whole story. Like I said in the radio shack, what you *can't* see or feel matters every bit as much as what you can.

"Such as?"

"Such as, when a change-up is coming. Even a small one can be a big deal. You need to read the signs of how fast it is coming, how intense it will be, how much it will alter your course."

"What signs? Everything out here is acting like itself. I don't see anything on the verge of changing…"

"It's *all* changing—all the time. Changes are pouring in every second. Your body is picking them up right now."

"Maybe *yours* is."

"Try this," I say, and hand him the mainsheet to the boom.

Stuart grips it too loosely and wind spills from the sail. He jerks the boom back and trims so close to the wind, we lose momentum. But after a few more minutes of that, he has steadied the boom and we are underway again.

"OK, now, can you feel the sail tugging on the rope you're holding?" I ask.

Stuart gives it a try. "I think so."

"There's a pattern to it. It's the pattern of tonight's midnight wind. You're feeling it break and form, break and form, over and over."

"Huh," he says.

"OK, now, the sea is making a pattern, too. Can you feel it in the way *2.0* is moving on the water?"

"You mean, the way her nose is pitching and yawing?"

"That would be the 'bow,' but yeah. That pitching and yawing is the pattern of the waves, forming and breaking, forming and breaking. Feel that?"

"Maybe…yes, there's a pattern."

"OK, here's the thing. Right now, we are inside an even bigger pattern. The wind is breaking and forming the sea's patterns, and the sea is breaking and forming the wind's patterns."

"You're losing me."

"Think of it this way. Your flight path runs right along the edge where the sea is becoming wind and the wind is becoming sea. Because that edge is pure movement. It's what is moving *2.0* right now. The world does its free running on that edge. It's where you'll find your handholds and footholds."

"You're joking, right? Liquid and air, going in every direction, that's all there is out here! Nothing to push off of. No footholds or handholds. There's nothing *close* to solid."

"You think wind and water aren't solid?" I reach for Stuart's hand, close it around the tiller, and let go.

He eyes the tiller he holds in one hand, then the mainsheet he grips in the other.

The breeze freshens, and *Home 2.0* lurches to starboard. First, Stuart lets out too much line. Then, he pumps the tiller back and forth, groping for control. Our makeshift boat reels and rolls.

"Stuart, try this. The rudder is your feet. The sail is your hands. The wind and water breaking and forming each other—they are your ledges and railings."

The fierceness of Stuart's grimace makes me think the lesson is over. But then, he readjusts himself on the seat.

His shoulders relax. His energy does what it did when he was preparing to sprint off the cliff. Stuart wills himself into that freerunning zone of his, right here on *Home 2.0*. And before long, he is finding shifts and changes in the wind and waves for her to grab hold of, push off of, and work together with. He is finding ways to keep *Home 2.0* going.

We sail across the surface of the tidal pool in elegant, easy figure eights. The moon's reflection drifts along with us in a long squiggly line from the new sandbar right up to the side of our boat.

I let my hand drag in the liquid moonlight. It has been days since my mind floated like this. And even though I have been talking the entire night with Stuart about anything and everything, I am wide awake. I can think of only one way to explain what just went down between me and Stuart: Our freaked-out selves were desperate to evolve new skills for surviving our equally freaked-out planet.

Out loud, I wonder, "Can you stop a force field from coming—after its waves get going?"

Stuart reaches up and peels strings of dried seaweed off of *2.0*'s patchwork sail. "Probably not," he says.

After a minute or two of puzzling it over, I say, "Maybe time is a force field. Maybe time has waves, and they carry forces from events that happened long ago into right now."

We reach the top of the figure eight. I talk Stuart through his first solo tack, and we head south again.

"At this very minute," I say, "the things we're doing could be sending waves of forces into the far future. All sorts of forces. Without us even knowing it."

In the silence that follows, I suspect I have lost Stuart. But, as he takes us through a lazy starboard turn, he must be considering my question. Because, after setting our new tack, he says, "Even if you can't stop a force field that is coming at you, with skill and luck, you might be able to surf it. And if you do, you get a chance to figure out what to make of where it's taking you."

Tapped in, he is.

In the midst of enjoying my contemplation of just how tapped in Stuart is, I realize that I have been staring absentmindedly at an odd, dazzling gleam on the predawn horizon.

"Sunrise," Stuart says, after following my gaze.

"Uh-huh."

But I'm not so sure.

"Let's head in," I say.

DAY THREE, AEC

 into exact alignment with the sun, I would have slept straight through Day Three, AEC. Last night's leapings off of cliffs and sailings on edges of change made it two all-nighters in a row for Stuart and me. It has taken a toll.

Pulling my blanket over my face does little to thwart the intensity of the post-fog sun. And even though I'm squeezing my eyelids shut, that strange light we saw off of *2.0*'s bow just before sunrise keeps drifting through my mind's eye. I'm sure we didn't dream it. But if it *was* something real…

I slither into a scrunched sitting position and squint through the porthole. Good. Things are looking surprisingly BEC this morning. Maybe Stuart is right and what happened the past two days was a temporary setback, a harsh but necessary course correction for our planet and its humans.

I lean against the sun-warmed wall of the bunk and savor

a tiny dollop of relief at the thought.

Here in the kitchen, wreckage from thrown together breakfasts covers the table and sink. Voices and tones of Morse Code drift in from the radio shack, sparking a second pulse of relief because—yeah—I have a few waking moments to myself.

When I stretch, my feet bump into something under the covers—my sketchbook. Which reminds me that Stuart called me a "human antenna" last night. I laugh out loud. This morning, "human slug" would be more like it.

Except, last night's unexpected adventures by land and by sea inspired a few precious flickers of curiosity and optimism, and there is nothing sluggish about how awake I grow as I wonder: What might happen if I let myself be what Stuart thinks I am? Full on. What might show up on this morning's blank page if I picked up my pen and summoned my inner antenna?

I open my sketchbook.

The screen door twangs.

Stuart looks in.

"You're awake," he says. He beelines for the kitchen table.

I can't believe he is this up and at it after all the energy we expended last night.

"We've been waiting for you, Ollie and me."

I close my sketchbook. So much for alone time.

"When I went running this morning, I caught Ollie sitting on the beach steps, crying. She said she dreamt that we'll be here forever."

He smears peanut butter across multiple slices of bread. "She just needs to have some fun," he concludes.

Heading over to my bunk, Stuart stacks two of the peanut butter sandwiches he just made and takes a voracious bite out of both at once.

"You'll need this," he says, chewing, and hands me the sandwich that is unbitten. "The parents are taking a beach walk to decompress. You have to help me cheer up Ollie. And we've got the perfect thing for that."

He's out the door before I can thank him for the dripping PB sandwich that I hold in my hand and am smitten by.

It has been days since I inspected myself in the mottled bathroom mirror. I hardly recognize the face I see. Not because of its back-to-back all-nighters. And not because of the sorry fact that it disentangled itself mere seconds ago from a grimy, rather sweaty, blanket. It's because—I'm staring at someone who I know I have met before, but she's so out of context, I can't place her. I knew this person, BEC. But here in AEC, I can't really say who she is.

I rearrange my hair. All that does is confirm my dire need for a haircut. The era of AEC is begging for something shorter. For now, I pull my hair back and go looking for a rubber band in the kitchen.

When I am finally put together enough to show myself in full sunlight, I walk outside to the sight of Stuart wheeling an egg-shaped tank out of the shack. And within minutes, it's obvious. There is no end to how much good clean fun you can serve up with a giant NOAA weather balloon.

Ollie quivers with excitement as Stuart unfurls the billowing whiteness from its storage bag. He connects the balloon's neoprene body to the helium tank and appoints me valve operator.

I take to my task like it's an essential public service. Soon, I'm inflating the flat form into a perfect, shining sphere that boasts very official NOAA logos and quickly expands to the size of an ice cream truck.

Stuart grabs the rope swinging beneath the balloon and clips his sportcam to it. He lets the tether slide through his hands until the bulbous body floats at least ten stories above our heads. When he turns the controls over to Ollie, her arms stretch above her head and the balloon raises her to her tiptoes. Beyond ecstatic, she keeps telling us how much she wants to climb the tether and measure the wind speed up there.

Blinding sunlight reflects off the orb as it soars above us. The glow it casts on our faces triggers my memory of the eerie whiteness Stuart and I saw this morning…hovering at the horizon…much too colorless to be a sunrise…much larger than any boat I can imagine, given how far away it was…glowing too brightly to be…

I look across the water. But the horizon is empty.

Ollie runs up to offer me a turn at piloting, and I park the memory. The balloon is sailing high and happy against a blue that is beyond blue. We need this good silly fun.

And so, we fly that spunky balloon, right up to the moment we can wait no longer to see what's on Stuart's sportcam.

Inside the radio shack, Stuart downloads video to his dad's laptop. I hit "play."

Jumping up and down, Ollie shouts, "There we are!"

On the screen, the ground falls away. Our video bodies fall away too, faces upturned and shimmering with excitement. Here in the shack, our physical selves bob and weave in front of the laptop with each swoop of the dangling camera.

As the balloon rises higher, jittery views of the lighthouse grounds grow more and more panoramic. Soon, we can see our whole island, and then, the ocean all the way to the horizon. We laugh and try not to get seasick—or I guess that would be balloon sick—from the camera's twirling.

"*Home 2.0* looks so small," I say.

"The higher we go," Stuart says, "the more East Ledge Island looks like the International Space Station floating in—wait. What is that? Go back."

"What is what? What do you see?" Ollie squeezes between us and the screen.

"I'm not sure," Stuart says.

I rewind the video.

"There!" Stuart says, and I hit "pause."

We examine the freeze frame. The camera is looking due east from at least ten stories above the island.

"I don't see anything," I say.

Stuart advances the video frame by frame until a blur on the horizon jogs into focus.

"There."

"That white smear?" I ask. "How did you even see that?"

"He wallpapered his bedroom with aerial views of the planets," Ollie sighs. "As if that's normal. And now he's got aerial view eyes."

I barely register what Ollie is saying because I'm

beginning to realize that, whatever this blur is, it is exactly where Stuart and I saw the odd glow this morning.

Stuart zooms in some more and hits "enhance."

"Holy shit," he says.

Center frame, a jagged mass of gleaming white has snapped into focus.

"It's bigger than this island," I say, as if that wasn't obvious.

"Awesome," Ollie whispers.

The entire human population of East Ledge is at the kitchen table, jammed around the laptop.

"But, why couldn't we see it when we were walking on the beach this morning?" Jennifer asks. "We can't see it from the kitchen window either."

"When you look for it from down here, it's below the horizon," Stuart says.

"Our balloon went so high, it could see around the curve of the earth." Ollie is breathless.

Mark walks to the kitchen window. "It *can't* be an iceberg. I did a model for that last month," he mutters.

Jennifer raises an eyebrow. "You were modeling icebergs?"

"The government is tracking the new ones north of here. Dozens of them. They're a hazard to the oil rigs. Estimates had them grounding off Nova Scotia. I never thought they would get this far south. Those prolonged storms in the North Atlantic this summer must have—"

I grab Dad's arm and stammer, "That wave—"

"I'm thinking the same thing, Kally," he says, studying

the video.

I step away from the screen. "It wasn't a rogue wave," I say. "A piece of this iceberg broke off and—"

"Oh, god," Jennifer hurries to join Mark at the window.

Stuart folds his arms and looks across the computer at me. "You knew this was out there."

I shake my head slowly. "I didn't—"

"Remember what you heard in the fog last night? 'Two echoes,' you said. One bouncing off the sea around the lighthouse, and one coming from farther out."

Stuart *was* listening to me go on about echoes last night.

"The second one was the foghorn bouncing off this iceberg," he concludes.

Ollie dashes into the sitting room and reappears carrying a pair of battered binoculars.

"I knew these would come in handy!" she says and darts out the door.

On the rim of the cliff, we pass the binoculars and take turns straining our eyes through their scratched lenses. Consensus comes easy. We are looking at an iceberg, all right. It's rising like the Earth's second moon, growing more visible on the horizon every minute—as shimmering and unbelievable as a mirage.

"It's moving fast," Stuart says.

"Fast enough to leave a wake." Dad passes the binoculars to Jennifer.

"How could it be this far south?" Jennifer asks, putting the binoculars to her eyes.

When my turn comes to see it close up, all I can offer is,

"It is way bigger than this island."

Ollie balances on her tiptoes to get a better angle on the horizon.

"Is it going to hit us?" she asks.

Now there's a question. Its shock wave jolts our assembly.

Jennifer's voice wavers as she asks, "Do you think the Coast Guard knows?"

"We can't call or even email until the internet is back," Stuart says. "It's been out for over 24 hours."

Mark puts his arm around his wife's shoulders.

"That means you're up, Jen."

I shuttle between the house and the shack with sandwich deliveries to Stuart's mom and everyone else. It has been hours, and Jennifer still can't get a reply to the nonstop calls she is putting out to Coast Guard and ham radio operators. "Iceberg" is spelled in dots and dashes on her notepad, ready to send. But no matter what frequency she uses, or which frenzied conversation of code she tries to break in on, the other operators won't slow down enough to catch her pleas.

I don't know Code, but the people on the radio who do sound freaked out to me.

With each sandwich run, I can tell that the iceberg has moved closer. By mid-afternoon, it has blotted out the eastern horizon all the way from ten o'clock to two o'clock. We seriously underestimated its size. It must be at least twice the length of our island.

I hand Stuart what must be his sixth sandwich of the day.

"Let's climb the tower," I say. "We can use the binoculars to measure the iceberg's speed and direction better from up there. Besides, the dots and dashes are making me—"

"Yeah, me too," he says.

We top the spiral staircase and lean out of one of the broken windows.

No longer resembling a formless ghost ship, the iceberg is fully recognizable for what it is: a massive landscape of starkly etched blue and white rising halfway between us and the horizon. It could be an artist's ice sculpture of a National Park mountain range.

On its north end, a glistening peak swoops upward six or seven stories before it angles off. The southern end is a jumble of cubes, spikes, and crevasses. In between, an odd expanse of reflected sunlight catches my attention.

Curious about what could be making the reflection, I raise the binoculars and gasp a sound I didn't know I could make.

"What do you see?" Stuart asks, hurrying to my side.

What I see is a gleaming blue-green arch spanning a massive void between the iceberg's two poles. It is the Brooklyn Bridge of ice bridges.

At a loss for words, I'm about to pass the binoculars to Stuart when something more catches my eye. Something white, but definitely not ice.

"Stuart, there's something *on* it." I squint through the fogged lenses.

"What sort of something?"

"Wait, there's a light under the bridge."

"What bridge?"

"It's flashing!"

I lower the binoculars and look at Stuart because—yeah—I need a reality check when I say, "There is a cruise ship stuck in the iceberg."

Stuart peers into my face as if I just spoke a language he doesn't understand. But then, the words sink in and—whatever that emotion is when panic meets cracking up? It erupts in both of us.

Stuart tries but fails to stifle a fit of nervous laughter as he takes the binoculars. Swinging them toward the iceberg, he sputters, "This is freaking insane!" But the instant he brings the scene into focus, his tone veers into full-on panic.

"Hey—Kally—that flashing. That's an *SOS*."

Stuart springs to the window that overlooks the grounds and wrestles it open.

On the lawn below, Ollie, Mark, and Dad are about to relaunch the balloon for a sportscam update on the iceberg.

"Ollie, get Mom!" Stuart shouts.

Ollie looks up at the tower. "She's still trying to find the Coast Guard on the radio."

Stuart shouts louder. "Just get her. Hurry."

I center the stuck cruise ship in the binoculars and say, "They attempted to sail under an ice bridge. Who *does* that?" I am in a state of massive disbelief of such stupid seamanship. Which makes it hard to have much sympathy for the ship's predicament, even as I inform Stuart, "They're still sending *SOS*. I guess we should try to signal something back."

When Stuart doesn't reply, I look to see why. He's studying the control panel for the lighthouse lantern.

"Too bad the beacon is automated. Otherwise, my mom could flash them an answer," he says.

A yellowed label on the lantern mounting catches my eye. "What about this?" I ask suggestively, and point to the faded, hand-printed words: "FOGHORN MANUAL OPERATION."

Stuart comes beside me to read the label. He grins.

I give him a look of warning.

He puts his fingers in his ears.

I press the button.

The entire tower quakes as it sends out its oh-too-familiar bellow.

Our respective family members squeeze in around us on the lantern room deck. I steady the binoculars against the windowpane to sharpen focus on the cruise ship. Stuart stands ready at the foghorn controls.

A scrap of notepaper trembles in Jennifer's hand. She takes a breath. "Here we go. Short—long—long. Short. Short—long—long. Short—short…"

Stuart sounds the foghorn according to Jennifer's score.

Ollie tugs her dad's arm, pulls his head to her face and says into his ear, "What is Mom saying to that stuck ship?"

Mark reads over Jennifer's shoulder. "We…will…send…help."

Jennifer calls out the final bits of code, and Stuart sends the last short blast of the horn resounding its way to the iceberg.

I push the binoculars into Jennifer's hands.

She trains them on the cruise ship.

We hold our collective breath.

"It's flashing!" she reports. "N — K — Y — O—"

"Thank you!" we shout in unison, and the lantern room erupts in whoops and high fives.

Back in the radio shack, after tense minutes of group pacing and giddy squirming, we fall silent. Jennifer has lowered the volume on the incoming din of Morse Code and pushed her chair back from the radio bench.

She massages her coding hand and says, "A few rounds of SOS sure got their attention." Glowing, she announces, "The Coast Guard is coming."

"You are amazing, you know that?" Mark gives her a hug.

The rest of us pile on the high fives and shoulder pats.

Everyone except Dad, that is. He's back to studying the iceberg from the shack's window.

"It has moved six miles closer since we first saw it." he says.

DISTURBANCE

WE STAKED OUT FRONT ROW SEATS on the beach, complete with blankets and folding chairs, and now we are taking turns squinting through the musty lenses of our antique binoculars. For the past hour, a dozen members of the U.S. Coast Guard have been transferring people dressed in various styles of cruise wear from the grounded—make that iceberged—ship, to the cutter.

"Hey, look!" Ollie shouts.

A safety orange motor lifeboat is buzzing away from the cutter and heading in our direction. As it speeds closer, we're able to make out the words painted on its side: "U.S. Coast Guard Rescue."

The pilot beaches her craft where our pier used to be and disembarks. Taking off her helmet, she comes over to shake hands. Her name tag reads "Seaman Taylor."

"Pleasure to meet you," Seaman Taylor booms. "I can't believe you reached us. Communication is a nightmare."

"My mom relayed *SOS* all around Canada," Ollie puffs out her chest.

"Well," Taylor says, "we just pulled 27 people off of that iceberg because you guys are amazing." She looks out at the rescue operation. "That ice bridge took out their communication antenna. If you hadn't been here…" She shakes her head at the ship in sharp disapproval, then looks back at us. "You all OK?"

"We're OK," Mark reports.

"Good." Taylor puts herself at ease. "I came over to assure you—we have you on our to-do list. Need anything?"

From the looks we exchange amongst ourselves, none of us can believe she asked that.

"Uh, we could use a lift home," Dad clues her in.

"For real?" Taylor is incredulous.

"Yes. For real," Stuart insists. "What we *need* is to get off this island as soon as possible."

Taylor looks even more disbelieving. "You been catching the news?"

"Stuart burned up the radio," Ollie blurts out.

"Long story." Mark takes Ollie by the shoulder and pulls her to his side.

"We got the satellite dish working again, but the internet is down most of the time," Stuart says. "So, no, we are not caught up on the news." His impatience is showing.

"Our phones don't work out here at all," Jennifer underscores.

Taylor checks her watch, looks over her shoulder at the cutter, then strides to the broken hull of *Home 2.0* and sits on it.

"Look, I'll make this quick. The grid is toast from the

East Coast to the Mississippi River—top of the country right down to the bottom. They took every last nuclear power plant off line this morning because of no guarantee of emergency backup power. There is a lack of electric power to gas and oil pipelines—and that has led to fuel shortages everywhere. The transportation grid is down because of historic flooding from the eastern mountains to beyond the Midwest, which wiped out bridges and closed interstates. East Coast cities are a mess—shortages of everything. People can't get in or out. Even if they did get out, there's nowhere for them to go that would make them better off. So, what I'm saying is, if you've got food and water…"

Taylor shrugs.

Sounding more than a little shell-shocked, Jennifer mumbles, "Well, like I told the Coast Guard person on the radio, I guess we have food for a week."

"The backup generator is running the lights and satellite dish. We have enough diesel for two weeks at least," Mark adds.

Taylor scans our lined-up faces and, ignoring the wall of chagrin she sees there, jumps up off *Home 2.0* and replies with a hearty, "Then I would stay put. There's a good chance you are the only ones on this end of the continent who are still on summer vacation." She looks out at the rescue scene. "And we've got our hands full. The minute we put in this evening, the town will have a hundred-plus new people who need everything." She turns back to us. "We'll be out this way again. Soon."

We just stand there.

She tries again. "Like I said, you're better off here. Trust me."

She heads for her craft.

"But my mom!" I call after her.

Taylor looks over her shoulder at me and then up at the lighthouse. "She isn't here?"

"She's in New York," Dad says.

"Are you in contact?"

"A few fragments of emails," Dad says. "She's trying to find a way to leave New York and get back to our home in Maine."

"That could take weeks," Taylor scoffs before catching herself. With a flash of sympathy in her voice, she quickly adds, "We just don't know."

"Can you help us get her back home?" I plead. "So that she will be there when we—"

"I don't see how I can help you with that. But I can have them unlock our ship's WiFi signal for as long as we are at the iceberg. Get on our signal. You can try emailing her."

She whips a notepad out of the pocket of her life vest and starts writing.

"And here's the email address for our communications officer back at the station. Petty Officer Yazzie. Tell him about your mother. I'll follow-up."

She hands me the slip of paper.

"Thank you," Dad says.

Pushing through the sand to her craft, Seaman Taylor calls over her shoulder. "I'll tell them to make sure they bring you a radio next time they're out here. But be advised—listening to it will promptly diminish any sense of vacation you have left."

Ollie runs alongside Taylor and asks, "Is the iceberg

going to hit our island?"

Taylor doesn't break her stride. "Its keel is already scouring East Ledge and we expect it to run aground before long. It won't get much closer than it is now. It'll be there for a while though—maybe all winter. Incredible, isn't it?" She stops to pat Ollie on the shoulder and says, "Enjoy it while it's here."

Taylor climbs into the lifeboat, starts the motor, and speeds away from shore. A hundred yards out, she turns a full circle while looking back at us through her mirrored helmet goggles.

I feel as small and abandoned as we must appear from out there.

She guns it, and her lifeboat churns away from our beach.

Dad surveys the ongoing rescue scene from the radio shack window. He's making sure the Coast Guard cutter is still anchored at the iceberg. As long as it's there, we can stay piggybacked on its super-fast and strong internet connection, which has us hooked up to email servers, news feeds—the entire world.

Turns out, that is not saying much. "The entire world" has shrunk to a few official government internet sites that still have power, plus the truncated, spasmodic emergency text messages.

"You sent their communications officer the address of the emergency center that Mom is at, right?" Dad asks.

"Just did. I'll keep on checking for anything new from her."

"Good going." He kisses the top of my head. "I need to eat, so do you. Don't get too caught up in reading the news. A short break won't hurt."

The door bangs shut behind him.

I am not hungry. And the only break I need is an email from Mom. It has been two days since her first message staggered through the broken grid to tell us that, at the moment she wrote at least, she was OK. I won't let myself think what could have happened since. So instead, I spend the next few minutes staring mindlessly at the laptop screen while obsessively hitting "get mail."

Scents of beach fire waft in through the door, and I decide that I *am* hungry after all. When I reach to close the laptop, it dings.

"Dad! It's Mom!" I shout. But he's out of earshot.

She sent the email to my account, addressed to me.

I attack the keyboard, rushing to download the whole message before the fragile connection between the Coast Guard cutter and New York City drops.

The message opens!

My heart races and my fingers tremble as I scroll and speed read. She is still OK, in the city, worried about us, wants to know where we are.

I can hear her voice in my head as I read. I don't want the email to end. I make myself read more slowly, even though I want to know everything she has to say—all at once.

I've had so much time to think, Kally. Your dad and I believed we should try to keep all of this as far away from you as possible for as long as we could. Now I know that we were wrong. We should have turned toward what's happening together. Please forgive me—

I blink back tears. I try to scroll, but there is nothing more to see.

Maybe her connection got cut off. Maybe she's going to send short messages one after the other, telegraph style, like she did the other night.

I hit "get mail" over and over. I want her voice to come back. I want to know what she's going to say next. Maybe what is happening will make sense or go away or turn out just fine *because of what she says next.*

The rainbow circle on the screen spins and spins and stops on nothing. Still, I can't let go of the split second of hope that glimmers each time I spin the circle again. So, I continue to beg the fragile thread that stretched for nanoseconds between me and my mother to reappear. Even if all I'm doing is calling down an empty satellite signal, at least I am doing something.

Suddenly, I burst out laughing at my own ridiculous self. Because here I am functioning—literally—as a human antenna.

The spell breaks. I pull my eyes away from the spinning circle. It's made me dizzy. And this radio shack is making me claustrophobic.

When I stand, I find myself looking out the window at one gargantuan iceberg that has been spit out by a prehistoric glacier in meltdown; one sorry cruise ship stuck onto said glacier specimen under an ice bridge that is big enough to count as a major piece of infrastructure—and is threatening to collapse any second; and one Coast Guard cutter uploading a hundred-plus cruise ship passengers, one at a time, out of bobbing orange rescue rafts.

It's surprising how *not* surprised I am that this bizarre

seascape actually exists right outside my window. In fact, it feels like déjà vu. Maybe it's the exhaustion, or maybe it's the adrenaline fatigue, but I stop fighting what I'm seeing. I simply give up expecting it to be something other than what it is. Which is not hard, because somewhere deep inside and beyond knowing—I felt this coming. The exact details about how and when Earth's unleashed tipping points would catch up to us might have escaped me. But that antenna Stuart says I have? It has been picking up that bigger picture just fine.

The sun set a few minutes ago and the sky is still bright. Everyone but me sits in a circle around the beach fire. From the top of the bluff, I watch Stuart skewer hot dogs for the celebratory picnic supper. A sweet onshore breeze carries the voices up the cliff.

Mark raises a beer and proclaims, "To a good day's work."

Dad toasts back, "To 127 rescued people."

Ollie waves her soda, "To the last can of pop."

Jennifer taps Ollie's shoulder and urges, "Ollie, concentrate if you want to do this. Now, 'O' for Ollie is…?"

"Easy. Long—long—long. Hey, they're leaving!" Ollie jumps up from the blanket and waves.

The vessel carrying Seaman Taylor, her mates, and the rescued victims of misguided tourism barrels away, abandoning the cruise ship to the epic fail that it has cued up for itself under the ice bridge. A minute later, the cutter disappears around the northern tip of our island.

In its wake, the moon peeks out from behind this slice

of Greenland's ice sheet.

Dad spots me standing on the top step and waves a plate of food in my direction. I'm not feeling as hungry as I was before Mom's email came. But I head down to the fire, anyway.

"Your hot dog," Dad bows gallantly. "Paired with the last eight chips on the island."

"There's a new email from Mom," I say. "Actually, she sent it this morning. She still hasn't gotten ours. She's really worried about us. But she's still saying that she's OK."

Dad lets out the breath he has been holding—for days, probably. "Thank god."

"Oh, Kally, I am so happy to hear that," Jennifer says.

"More reason to celebrate," Mark says.

I can see now how worried Dad has been, and I rush to add: "Mom said she's trying hard to find some way to get home."

Dad nods. He's still offering up the plate of food. I consider the festive picnic scene and the less than festive hot dog.

"Thanks, but I think I'll take a walk," I say.

A few dozen yards down the beach, the sound of Ollie's delighted laughter makes me turn and look back at the fire. It's lighting up everyone's eyes. Stuart is looking out over the water with an amazing expression on his face. It reminds me of the look people get when they become transfixed by the most beautiful painting in the museum.

Following his gaze, I see the moon, rising behind a pinnacle of ice. It's as if the iceberg carved a perfect circle from itself and floated it up into the sky.

When I look back at Stuart, he's not looking at the

iceberg moon anymore. With that amazing expression still on his face, he's looking at me.

I take my time walking deeper into the dusk toward the far southern end of our beach, and the wall of boulders that stands between us and New York City.

Without warning, the sound-feeling rises from the sand under my feet. I had almost forgotten about it in the craziness of today. But tonight, it's even more intense, and closer.

I kneel just out of the surf's reach and tilt my ear to the sand. From this angle, I can't tell if what I'm feeling is coming from the earth below me or from somewhere out at sea. A breeze sweeps across my ears. It's enough to brush the sound-feeling away. When the wind slackens, I listen again, but whatever it is, it has withdrawn again.

I look back up the beach at the picnic. In the blue-grey moonlight, it takes a few seconds for me to distinguish Stuart, striding toward me. He's silhouetted against the fire and carrying the plate of food I rejected.

I scoop a handful of the wet sand and hold it up to the darkening sky. Stuart does a double take at the sight of the blue-white lights blinking spasmodically in my hand.

I stand, take the plate of food from him, and place my fistful of twinkling stars on his palm.

"They're marine plants. Doing what fireflies do," I say.

Stuart cups the sand carefully with both hands.

"I've heard about this! Bio-something, right?"

"Bioluminescence. These little guys do great things for the ocean. There aren't many of them left around here because of how warm the water…anyway, they light up whenever something disturbs them."

"Why do they think that's a good idea?" he asks.

"It's weird, right? Unless you imagine yourself being one of them."

"I'm game." Stuart grins.

"All right. Imagine a fish is hanging around, getting ready to eat you. How do you feel?"

"Disturbed?"

"Very. So, you light yourself up, hoping that an even *bigger* fish will spot your flashing 'here I am' sign and head on over to eat you."

"I do?"

"Yes, because you're also hoping that, while the bigger fish is swimming in your direction—"

"I get it. While the *bigger* fish is on its way over to eat me, it spots the *smaller* fish that was coming for me in the first place—and eats *him* instead." Stuart studies the blinking in his hands for a moment, and concludes, "Brutal, but smart."

I scoop up another handful of sparkles. "Except, these little guys are confused right now. They're not blinking because a hungry fish is after them; they're feeling disturbed because of how these waves are crashing them into the sand."

"So, you're saying they want to lure a big fish over here so that it will eat all this disturbing sand?" Stuart asks.

"Basically. How futile is that?" I let the fistful of sea creatures slide from my palm back into the water and hand the untouched plate of food back to Stuart.

"You OK?" he asks.

I do not wish to discuss how *not* OK I am. "You smell

like a campfire," I say instead.

He winces and says, "So do you."

"No, it's good. It smells like—you know—good times."

"You should eat," Stuart lectures.

Examining Stuart's moonlit plate of charred hot dog and damp chips, I shake my head.

In the time we've been focusing on the twinkling sand, the tableau that captivated Stuart earlier has turned even more dreamlike. It captures both of us now. The entire spectacle of moon, horizon-obliterating iceberg, and doomed cruise ship looks like it's being lit from within, in a bioluminescent way.

"How can something so…wrong be so…enchanting?" I ask.

"The iceberg might be enchanting—but that cruise ship is deeply absurd," Stuart says.

I try to muster an ironic smile, but I don't quite make it.

"See that satellite?" Stuart points to a speck of light gliding between stars. "It's looking at our iceberg. And in the stream of data it just beamed down, it embedded a big red warning light because it detected a pattern change: A hunk of the Arctic is not where it should be."

Stuart crouches at the water's edge and waits for the next wave. When it slides in, he gently disperses the blinking sand universe he has been holding.

"But there is no power at that satellite's receiving station. And there is no NASA to act on the warning it just sent." He watches the sparkles spread in the lapping water. "A baseless satellite, running on automatic, sending data to nowhere. How futile is *that*?"

Stuart stands and steps back from the water.

"Really, feel free *not* to try to cheer me up," I say.

So, we default into silence, and scan the otherworldly seascape before us. Glistening bits of the iceberg's body parade past the sandbar off our beach.

"Unbelievable," Stuart says under his breath, sounding more tired than amazed.

"Sometimes, I think it's talking to us—in a voice without words," I hear myself saying, matter-of-factly. Stuart looks at me sideways, and I cringe at how crazy that just sounded, even for a human antenna.

But before I can explain or take it back, the scream of a military jet takes away my breath and we duck heads as it blasts to the southeast.

A second later, two black triangles screech past, barely clearing the top of our lighthouse, and blast toward the horizon. Before we can react to that, three helicopters in formation pound in from the north and follow the jets.

I grab the sleeve of Stuart's sweatshirt and pull him with me, back toward the rising sparks of the beach fire. Our family members are unfolding themselves from duck and cover positions. On our right, an enormous block of ice surfs its way toward the picnic. Shining with borrowed moonlight, it lunges up and forward with each swell. Silent lightning snakes above the horizon.

DAY FOUR, AEC

DAD AND MARK HAVE TAKEN UP POSITIONS on either side of the coffee pot. From the looks of them, if they slept at all last night, their dreams were haunted.

Ollie straggles in from the sitting room and over to the kitchen table. Unusually quiet, she plops into a chair next to her brother. He's holding a coffee cup and staring down at the AM radio that got fried yesterday morning. No one bothered to remove its crisped body from the kitchen table, and it has turned into a sad memorial to itself.

Dark thoughts seem to be plaguing everyone.

Here under my blanket, I have failed to achieve any sort of thought at all beyond a few vague memories of last night's events: being startled awake over and over by jets screaming both far in the distance and right overhead; sounds of multiple helicopters thrumming in all directions; getting shaken in my bunk by cracks of thunder that never brought rain. Yesterday's rescue celebration seems like it happened ages ago.

The simple act of remembering is exhausting. I'm sure I would have fallen back to sleep if Jennifer's anxious cry hadn't shot through the kitchen.

"Mark? Mark!" Jennifer flings open the screen door.

At the sight of Stuart and Ollie, she forces a smile and stops to catch her breath.

"Well. You all slept in. Didn't you? That's good. Good." She fidgets with the fistful of scribbled notes she is clutching.

Stuart is far from fooled. "Mom, what is going on? Every time I woke up last night, you were at the radio with the headset on."

"I'm sorry if I woke you up. I couldn't sleep. So, I was…trying to get my coding speed up."

"Not buying it." Stuart says. "Whether you talk to us about it or not, we have to live it. The Pact covers all of this now."

Coming to life, Ollie plunks down her cereal spoon. "Yeah, you promised."

Still holding his mother's gaze, Stuart reaches over and smooths Ollie's hair.

Jennifer's strained smile shape-shifts to a genuine glow of admiration for her kids. She exchanges a shrug of surrender with Mark and walks to the center of the room. Straightening her back, she shuffles the scraps of paper and sighs. "All those things Seaman Taylor said about what was happening—it was just too hard not knowing—but the internet still wouldn't work—and everybody on the ham radio was coding so fast, it took me all night to catch these few words…"

I pull myself upright as the bunk space allows and gather the blanket in around me as Jennifer starts to read from the slips of paper.

"Electricity rationing. Freeways like campgrounds. Grid refugees—whatever that is. Gas shortages. They're trying to get a radiation leak outside New York City under control."

I send Dad a panicked look.

From across the room, he says, "Mom is with resourceful people, Kally, and she knows the city very well."

"You think any of that makes a difference?" I ask, genuinely stunned. He still has not accepted the glaring fact that some AEC emergencies can't be so-called managed.

More military jets rumble in the distance, spiking the tension in the kitchen. We wait for their growls to fade away, then turn back to Jennifer.

She flips to her next note and, just as she's about to read, the air inside the kitchen—and inside our chests—pounds violently.

We spill out of the house and shield our faces from the stinging blasts of sand. A 20-foot-long, bulbous orange and white Coast Guard transport helicopter beats the air above our heads. A man in an orange Coast Guard jump suit descends from its belly in a basket. When he's a few feet above the ground, he jumps out and jogs toward us.

"Good morning," he shouts above the deafening thwaps. "Ensign Brooks," he says and points to his name tag. "They didn't give me your names."

Dad shouts, "David Guthrie. Kally, my daughter."

Jennifer calls out, "Jennifer Hart, this is my husband,

Mark. And this is Stuart. And Ollie."

Stuart and I exchange incredulous looks. The parents are acting like we're at a weekend social party even though, right next to us, a helicopter is lowering a metal container the size of a tool shed stenciled with thick black letters that say: FEMA DISASTER RELIEF.

"Honored to meet you," Brooks yells. "The whole station is talking about you. Getting those people off that iceberg was the first happy ending we've had in days."

It doesn't take him long to see that, despite their cheery handshakes, the people in front of him haven't begun to process his aerial arrival, much less the FEMA container that just landed next to them.

"OK. I better make this fast. So, listen hard." He pulls a laminated card from his pocket and reads.

"*By the authority of the President of the United States, you are hereby conscripted into National Service, Civilian Emergency Corps.*"

He stops and looks at us.

"Your commanding officer is Captain Joan Vasquez. Your headquarters is the East Ledge Coast Guard Station—that's where we're from. Your site of deployment is East Ledge Light." He looks around at the grounds. "This place is more important than ever."

We are not looking impressed. We are looking more than a little stressed on account of the nonstop pounding of helicopter blades, the frenetic lowering of even more containers and—yeah—what Ensign Brooks just said.

He resumes reading. "*I am Ensign Brooks. I will be in charge of supplying this post and delivering the Captain's orders. You will report to me, using this.*"

He fishes in his cargo pocket, pulls out a walkie talkie,

and presents it to us. Jennifer hesitates, then reaches for it. Brooks nods.

"Your orders are as follows. Staff the East Ledge Lighthouse. Ensure that its light and horn are fully operational at all times. Establish regular watches. Report all events of interest, such as approaching storms—"

He looks up at us. "The official weather reports are fundamentally unreliable." He looks back down at the card, *"—approaching storms, dense fog, and all other conditions potentially dangerous to ships and navigation. In addition, you will report all sightings of ships or watercraft that are not of the United States Coast Guard."*

He looks up again and addresses the parents.

"People are trying to reach Canada in small boats. If you see anything like that, call us. It's dangerous. It's illegal. We'd be setting up a blockade if we didn't have everything else to do." He goes back to reading. *"Report any unusual phenomena—"* He looks up, "you know, gigantic schools of sharks, floating plastic islands, methane fireballs, fish die-offs, red tide, meteotsunamis, tidal maelstroms, glacier collapse tsunamis—"

Ollie's eyes light up. "That stuff's happening?"

Brooks points to the walkie talkie clutched in Jennifer's hand. "Anything like that happens, you call me."

He pockets the card he's been reading. "Now, do you understand these instructions?"

Six heads jerk up as if they are about to nod "yes," but not one of us manages to pull it off.

The FEMA containers lined up on the ground now total three. Finding his voice, Mark points to them and says, "What is all that?"

"Food, propane, emergency drinking water, blankets, warm clothes, snow boots—we had to guess on sizes."

Jennifer reaches out and grabs a handful of Mark's shirt sleeve. "Snow boots?"

"Are we in the army?" Ollie trills.

Addressing Ollie, Brooks reiterates, "Like I said, you're in the National Service. Civilian Emergency Corps. Under the command of the United States Coast Guard."

"Awesome," Ollie says, gazing at Brooks with admiration.

"I don't get it. What the hell is going on back there?" Stuart glares at the descending fourth container stamped: COMFORT KITS.

"Oh, right," Brooks says. "They said you didn't have a radio."

"Yeah! Seaman Taylor said you guys would bring us one," Ollie informs him, as if she is one of his gang now.

"If we did, it would be in one of these." Brooks walks over to the nearest FEMA container and kicks it. His walkie talkie screeches. He looks up and waves to the pilot in the chopper overhead.

Turning back to us, he drops the military-speak.

"Look, you know the power grid is down everywhere from the Eastern Seaboard to Denver, right? Last night we got word that even if they *could* restore it close to normal, it would take years."

"Years!?" six voices call out in various combinations of shock, outrage, and bewilderment.

Then, Jennifer nods knowingly, "Grid refugees."

"Correct," Brooks says. "That's what the news is calling folks east of the Mississippi who are heading west for electricity. But they've got that megadrought in the plains, and power shut offs on the west coast to prevent wildfires. Even without the fires, there is nowhere near enough drinking water or shelter for evacuees. The president took over the railroads. They're filling tanker cars with water from Lake Michigan and hauling it west. And now there's the data center brownouts—big headache—people are panicking over their bank accounts and records. Around here, we're dealing with waterborne disease outbreaks in the cities, displaced animals and insects coming in from the outskirts in search of food, survival looting pretty much everywhere, rogue icebergs grounding in major harbors and growlers obstructing shipping lanes—

"Growlers! What are growlers?" Ollie asks.

"Broken off chunks of icebergs, bad for ships—hard to see on radar in high seas."

Brooks looks out over our bluff at the iceberg, then at his watch. He lets out a loud sigh.

"What else don't you know…early this morning, Wall Street crashed big time. Probably because the president declared martial law yesterday, did I say that already? He gave us an entirely new border to enforce: the Mississippi River. No one can cross it except on official business. People are going to have to stay put and make it work where they are."

"You mean, you expect us to stay *here*?" I ask. Suddenly, East Ledge Island feels like the tiny castaway of rock that it is.

"What he means is, we're drafted," Stuart spits.

Brooks senses a potential resister and says, gently, "You have been conscripted into National Service because we need you. Because you can help. Because you have proven capable."

"Like I said," Stuart mutters.

Ensign Brooks pivots and strides toward the dangling basket that waits to lift him to the transport helicopter.

"Check out what you've got here and make sure you ask for a radio if you don't find one in these," he says as he strides past the four hulking FEMA containers. "Draw up a list of whatever else you need. Use that walkie talkie to inform me of your top priorities. We'll try our best to get back here sometime next week—or the week after."

He pivots again, drill sergeant style, and faces the new keepers of East Ledge Light.

"Understood?" he hollers.

I step forward and shout above the helicopter's whirlwind. "My mom—"

"Oh, right!" Brooks snaps his fingers. "Officer Yazzie received your email with that info on her. Captain Vasquez has a son in New York. She was able to get ahold of him and he said he'd try to find your mother."

Dad reaches for my hand and squeezes it.

Brooks smiles and says, "He'll make sure your mother knows you're here. We're doing our best. OK? OK."

Ollie runs up to him, tugs the back of his shirt, and shouts, "I'm a spotter."

Brooks gives her a long look, then he calls over to Mark and Jennifer. "Is that serious? Does she need medical—"

"She's a *weather* spotter," Jennifer calls back, sounding like she has had to explain it many times. "For NOAA. Officially."

"No kidding," Brooks looks at Ollie with newfound

respect. "Well, now you're a weather spotter for the United States Coast Guard. I'll inform Chief Forecaster Williams. She'll appreciate reports."

Ollie runs back to Mark and Jennifer, her face beaming.

Brooks climbs into the basket and shouts even louder as it levitates to the helicopter. "If that ice bridge collapses, or if the iceberg wobbles or flips over or anything like that, head to the top of the lighthouse."

He disappears into the chopper's belly. As it banks and thrums north, he reappears at the open door and salutes.

We stand there.

The aircraft shrinks to a speck and a whole new level of crushing isolation closes in around us.

Jennifer looks from the lighthouse to the mountains of ice just off our shore, then back to the lighthouse. Her eyes climb the tower, and she says, haltingly, "Maybe we should start sleeping up there?"

It has been several hours since Ensign Brooks' visitation. At first, we tried to sit still at the picnic table and convince our stomachs to accept their overdue breakfasts. But, turns out, large containers of FEMA disaster supplies generate potent fields of anxiety in humans.

Dad must have recognized early warning signs of disaster fatigue in the ways we were pushing cereal around in our bowls. It motivated him into full-on emergency manager mode. That, plus his relief at knowing the Coast Guard is attempting to find Mom, has made him out-and-out energetic. His first act after giving up on breakfast was to assign Stuart and me to his inventory team. And now, according to his instructions, we're bucket-brigading the immediately useful-for-daily-life stuff out of the FEMA containers and sorting it into categories around the picnic table.

So far, we recorded tallies of military food rations, water purification tablets, light sticks, survival blankets, duct tape rolls, propane canisters, batteries, toolkits, medical supplies, hand-held solar chargers and—yeah—snow boots. Next, we'll consolidate all the industrial-strength gear—lifeboats, tents, chain saw, water distiller, composting toilet—and store it in the green FEMA container, aka "the garage."

I duck through the hatch of the near-empty yellow container and head for its dark recesses. My steps echo in the hollowness where the last zip-tied roof-replacement rain tarp awaits transfer to the garage. Standing over it, I listen to the metallic echoes of my breathing in the belly of a steel whale that swallowed FEMA stockpiles, and now, me.

Dad's voice drifts in through the hatch. He's explaining something about solar chargers to Stuart.

I guess Dad is doing exactly what he taught people in emergency management to do: "trust the training but expect the unexpected." If I had his training, maybe I would be trusting it too. Like him, I could be kicking into first responder mode. But I don't, and I'm not. *No* training, not even Dad's, could tell a person how to respond to the planet-wide emergencies that are underway. They are undreamt of.

So—yeah—here we are, fully *untrained* for Reality, AEC and fully conscripted into being first responders to whichever of its unimaginable new circumstances swarm ashore.

I stoop to lift the armload of tarps and decide that Dad's motto requires an immediate update. "Trust the training but expect the unexpected" doesn't cut it anymore. From now on, my motto is *Trust nothing you thought you knew. Expect only the unexpected.*

FRAGILE TIME

FINISHED WITH COUNTING AND RECORDING the tally of 288 aluminum cans labeled DRINKING WATER, I pop one open, change that number to 287, and sit down at the picnic table.

As of this morning, the home screen is the only part of my phone that works. Each time I check to make sure Mom's photo is still there, it has degraded by another few thousand pixels. Now, the only thing I'm able to recognize is her bracelet. I trace the blue string of beads with my fingertip, and yet another new reality of life, AEC, gets its turn to sink in: *I don't know when I will see her again.*

Crinkling up the empty aluminum can, I compel my mind to change subjects from agonizing over how much I miss my mom to—sure, why not—agonizing over the fact that the packaging these disaster supplies came in is a garbage crisis in the making.

Speaking of which, over at the bright yellow FEMA

container, Jennifer is pondering a pair of the arctic-worthy snow boots that Ensign Brooks delivered. As she runs her hand along the fur trim, I can't tell if she is about to laugh or melt down.

On the other side of the battered blue FEMA container, Ollie is spinning the cups of the wind speed instrument.

"Next time the internet is on, can I message my friends?" she asks.

Dangling the boots by their laces, Jennifer hurries over to Ollie and gives her a hug.

"Of course you can."

"Can I call Gramps, too?"

"That's the first call we'll make."

Stuart has been rummaging inside the final FEMA container to be inventoried. He emerges carrying a bulky pack of brown, shrink-wrapped wads labeled: MEAL, READY-TO-EAT, INDIVIDUAL.

"Here, Ollie," he says. "Open this and tell us what's for supper."

Ollie takes the bundle and bends under its weight, frowning.

"Buck up," Stuart laughs, "you're a Coast Guard ground truther."

"She's a what?" I ask.

Ollie springs back to life. "Ground truthing! It's what all the weather spotters do. We verify weather situations by experiencing them firsthand on the ground."

"Oh," I say.

Biting her lip, Jennifer scans the growing piles of uncrated supplies. "Do you think that we should try to email their schools?" she asks Mark.

"The last time the internet was up, they were saying something about schooling in place," I announce, before resuming renew my attempts to make sense of the "flameless ration heater" that I can see tucked between the wads of "meals" in the package that Ollie holds.

"They actually called it that? 'Schooling in place?'" Stuart asks, sounding annoyed.

"Does that mean no school?" Ollie pipes up.

"No, it means all of this," Mark sweeps his arms wide, "is school now."

"Awesome," Ollie whispers.

A few minutes later, Stuart finishes his inventory of the white FEMA container and, blinking, steps out of it, into the sunlight.

"That's it. And still no radio. But *these* will be great for whoever's on watch." He displays an impressive pair of military binoculars.

"That's me!" Ollie drops the bundle of rations and jumps to claim the binoculars. Nabbing the walkie talkie from the picnic table, she makes a run for the lighthouse—only to be shortstopped by her father.

"I'll hold on to this," Mark says, freeing the walkie talkie from her clutches.

"But I might see something," Ollie protests.

"And then, I will help you call it in," Mark says.

Ollie trudges toward the lighthouse, the binoculars swinging heavily from her shoulder.

Dad folds his arms across his chest and inspects the piles arrayed across the table and lined up in loose categories on the lawn.

"OK," he says, "let's figure out where to put these

supplies so they are protected from the weather."

"The radio shack has that storage room—"

Stuart is interrupted by Ollie's shouts from the base of the lighthouse tower.

"How big does it have to be before it's an iceberg?" she asks.

Offshore, dozens of growlers as big as subway cars have appeared, riding in the currents that skirt our island.

I pry open the salt-encrusted window in the radio shack's storage room and gulp fresh air. A breeze hasn't diluted the musty smells of this room in ages. Bands of sunlight streak in too, painting luminous stripes across dancing motes of dust.

Stuart avoids my eyes as he comes through the doorway balancing a pyramid of shrink-wrapped, FEMA-regulation toilet paper. We set to rearranging wooden crates and curious, rusty objects on the plank shelves that hang from the wall. We need to make room for the supplies waiting on the lawn. But it's difficult to stay on task. The ancient treasures are enthralling.

One by one, to the dusty sunbeams, we hold up keepers' ledgers, decades-old magazines, framed paintings of seascapes, a typewriter, coils of handmade rope, a brass sextant, fishing gear. I can't wait to show Dad the hand-sewn sail we found. We could use it to give *Home 2.0* a major upgrade.

A glint of light reflects off of something tucked between the rafters. Stuart pulls down a cobwebbed bottle of wine. Vintage, 1922.

Behind a trunk covered with sand dust, I find a faded painting of an idyllic, springtime meadow. I keep going back to it until, finally, I set it aside. I know just the place for it inside my bunk cave.

Reluctantly, Stuart and I tear ourselves away from our treasure hunt and resume clearing space in the center of the room. We finish just in time to receive deliveries of shrink-wrapped blankets and military style wool sweaters via the two dads. We ferry in what is left from outside while Dad records names and tallies on his official storeroom list.

The only person spared inventory duty is Jennifer. She volunteered to be first up on Dad's new lookout schedule, and now, she's multitasking in the radio room. Through the window, she monitors the iceberg and the bits of horizon it hasn't blocked, while, at the bench, she works the Morse Code key—more fluidly than ever.

From inside the storeroom, I see Ollie enter the shack and hang a calendar above the weather instrument monitors. It's from a marine supply outfit.

"This was in the kitchen," she says, "but I need it here for my weather logs. When did we get here?"

"Um…Saturday, the 17th," Jennifer says.

I watch Ollie circle August 17, then cross off the next three days while Jennifer sits back in the radio operator's chair and removes her headset. She's glowing.

"I just relayed a message for someone who needed drinking water," she tells Ollie.

"I bet you get a medal," Ollie declares.

"Everybody needs some sort of help," Jennifer says, sounding like she didn't hear Ollie. She shakes her head, dutifully scans the horizon outside the window, then dons her headphones again and picks up her pencil.

It's still an hour before sunset, but already the sky and mountain range of ice off our shore are the color of rust. I'm sitting on the bottom of the beach steps, trying to draw a scientific illustration of the iceberg.

This afternoon's lookout duty is making me feel great and bummed out all at the same time. Great, because I'm experimenting with a way of drawing that I have not attempted since I was in second year art class. Bummed, because of what sitting for hours with—yeah—an iceberg, has got me thinking. I'm realizing that while our bodies may have crash landed here in AEC, our heads are still in the clouds of BEC. The six of us haven't paused for a second to let our heads catch up. Instead, we spent the first day of our newly conscripted lives robotically emptying FEMA containers. Sure, we checked off the tasks at the top of Dad's to-do list. And, yeah, he successfully kept his disaster victims too busy to even consider freaking out. But that only means the hard work of freaking out is still ahead.

Maybe Dad needs to put *that* on the list of things to do.

A waft of chilled air grazes my cheek. At first, I can't believe it. But soon, I'm certain. I'm feeling the iceberg!

I smile involuntarily, set down my pen, and stretch my arms above my head. Time to perform another 180-degree scan of the horizon from north to south. At least, the part of it that is still visible on either side of the iceberg.

The only thing my efforts turn up is Stuart, freerunning along the boulders at the far end of the beach. I reach for the souped-up military binoculars, hesitate, then train them on Stuart anyway.

The quarter of a mile between us shrinks to inches. I've caught him in the middle of executing a combination vault up onto the tallest boulder followed by a somersault down to the sand. He lands like his feet are wearing anti-gravity shoes. Then, without skipping a beat, he pivots, meets my eyes right through the binoculars—and flashes a self-satisfied grin.

I yank the binoculars down from my eyes and pick up my pen. It isn't long before I hear Stuart calling out, "You're on watch. You're supposed to be surveilling our watery perimeter, not your fellow conscripts." His voice is smiling as he runs towards me.

"Small island," I call back without looking up from my sketchbook.

He slows to a walk and pulls up alongside to see what I'm drawing.

"Hey, that actually looks like an iceberg. You *can* draw."

It strikes me that this is the first time Stuart has teased me or anybody else. He's simply not the teasing type.

"Somebody might need to know how a rogue iceberg acts when it's this far from home," I say.

"Field notes!" he declares. "From the strange and wholly unexplored new world of this—our final frontier. Where Civil Emergency Corps conscripts boldly go where no one has gone before, seeking out new life and new civilizations—"

"Besides, I enjoy looking at it," I interrupt.

Stuart ignores my irreverence for what has got to be his favorite sci-fi show, and squats next to me.

"When I was stacking the last of the so-called comfort

kits in the storeroom, I found a beat-up box filled with these." He pulls a small square of cardboard out of his leg pocket.

It takes me a second to recognize what it is that he's holding. A photographic slide!

I pinch the corner of its frame between my fingers and lift it to the sunset.

"I found a projector, too," my fellow conscript reveals.

Mark tacks a bed sheet to the side of the radio shack while Dad runs an extension cord to the 60-year-old slide projector. The rest of us sit in eager anticipation, scattered across the grass on brand new FEMA blankets. We are consuming buckets of fresh popcorn thanks to Jennifer's dwindling but still remarkable stash of original vacation food—which she has firmly placed under her exclusive control.

That bottle of 1922 wine rests in the center of the food blanket. It has been lovingly dusted and ceremoniously placed.

"It's dark now!" Ollie hollers.

"A little longer," Jennifer admonishes.

Ollie resumes making notes in her weather log. Without looking up, she asks no one in particular, "What is that sound, anyway?"

My eyes dart to Ollie's face.

"What sound?" Mark asks.

"*Now* what?" Jennifer sits bolt upright and scopes out the grounds.

"Shh," Ollie says.

I hold my breath. Everyone is watching Ollie as she cocks her head. "That!" she says.

I rise to my feet slowly.

Mark strains his ears, then concludes, "I don't hear anything."

Dad shakes his head, "Neither do I."

I inch closer to Ollie, scrutinizing her every expression as she peers over her left shoulder, then her right.

"It sounds like…growling," she says.

"*Muffled* growling, right?" I ask.

"Kind of."

Now Stuart is looking at the sea, too. "It feels like a truck dragging an axel through potholes," he says.

"Yeah." Ollie jumps up off her blanket and rubber necks over the cliff.

"Mark?" Jennifer says, groping anxiously for his arm.

I, however, am feeling less anxious than at any other moment, AEC. Stuart and Ollie are having the sound-feeling. It's not just me. The sound-feeling is *real*.

"Do you hear it?" I ask my dad.

The adults pull themselves up off their blankets and face the ocean. They listen closely—but shake their heads.

"Whatever they are hearing, it's below the range of our 40-something ears," Dad tells Jennifer and Mark.

"Wait," I say, my voice trembling with simultaneous excitement, relief, and fear. "I tried to draw it when I was on watch this afternoon."

I run to my blanket, snatch up my sketchbook, flip to the last page, and hold it high above my head.

"It sounds like *this*," I say.

Heavy, jagged lines drip black ink down the page. They

curve back on themselves over and over, tangling in four dimensions, through all space and time.

At the lip of the dune cliff, we gather around Ollie. The parents are holding my drawing of the sound-feeling at arm's length and viewing it with palpable dread and confusion. Ollie is holding the walkie talkie high in the air, earpiece pointed to the sea.

Barely breathing, Ollie, Stuart and I listen, then let out a simultaneous, "There!"

Ollie wrenches the walkie-talkie out of the air and shouts into the microphone, "That's it. Did you hear it?"

There's a long pause. Then, the voice of Ensign Brooks squawks from the walk talkie.

"No. But your mic is picking up something. We can see it on our meter."

Another pause.

"OK. We'll try to identify it. If it changes, call us. In the meantime, its code name is 'Ollie.'"

Ollie's eyes couldn't be wider. She reality-checks each of our faces to make sure she is not dreaming as we shower her with congratulatory hugs and pats.

Every ten seconds, our robotic time machine squeaks, grinds, and advances its carousel of slides, sending the next photo clunking into place in front of the smoking lamp.

The white sheet on the outside wall of the shack furls in the breeze, animating snapshots of everyday life: ships, storms, garden flowers, holidays, birthdays. The

Kodachrome colors are vivid and vibrantly alive.

In one slide, the keeper's family stands on the exact spot where we are sitting right now on our FEMA blankets.

We laugh and offer running commentaries on the '60s and '70s clothes and hairstyles worn by the strangers we are meeting, and getting to know, through this portal in time. And everyone, including Ollie, savors sips of wine from the bottle that someone in these photos might have touched.

But it's not long before our laughter dies away. The people looking out of the photos at us from half a century ago do not understand how fragile their way of life is. Their faces show no awareness that their children and grandchildren will live on an achingly different planet. The last thing they could imagine looming off their shore is a hunk of Greenland big enough to hold a small town. And for sure, they never pictured having four FEMA containers lined up on their front lawn.

When the final slide pops back into the carousel, the white square of projected light is blinding.

"I wonder what it's like everywhere else tonight?" Mark blinks at the blank bedsheet. "Is everyone, everywhere, furiously gathering data, stunned and groping for what to do next?"

"It's like we're in that game," I say, stretching. "The one where you walk around like normal until someone shouts 'freeze.'"

"Freeze tag," Ollie informs me.

"Except, wherever you are right now, you'll be frozen there for years," Stuart says, tossing popcorn into the air and catching it in his mouth. He must see the horror that floods my face, because he quickly leans toward me. "Oh, no, I don't mean your mom, Kally."

I pull my phone out of my pocket. When I press the power button, the screen glows empty white, like the sheet rippling in front of us. "It's OK. It's just, a little while ago, the salt finally got to the rest of her picture," I say.

Jennifer and Mark shake out their blankets. They're on watch tonight, and they invited Ollie to sleep next to them in the tower. Yawning, Ollie follows them to the lighthouse, her blanket dragging behind her.

When the projector fan switches itself off, I'm able to pick up the sound-feeling, aka The Ollie. It has been a constant companion this evening. Our mystery guest.

Dad sends the projector cycling through the slides once more, drowning out The Ollie. He pours the last of the wine into his glass and grows still. People flare to life on the fluttering bedsheet—and then disappear, just as quickly.

I lie flat on the grass to watch the stars. On his blanket, Stuart does the same.

Soon, I'm brooding over the question Mark dared to speak earlier. What *is* it like everywhere else tonight? Have we six humans on East Ledge won whatever game of freeze tag this is—or have we lost? Is it wrong to feel lucky that I'm out here on this island with enough government-issued emergency supplies to sustain a village? Is it bad to feel that I am missing something big and important by not being in the heart of it all, like Mom is? Instead of drawing icebergs, shouldn't I be helping people who got freeze-tagged in parts of the world where they are having to work way harder than we are, just to survive?

The questions don't stop.

But for the moment, at least, they slip out of the

dreamscape that this night has become…and into sleep…
as I lie…side by side…on the grass, with Stuart.

DAY FIVE, AEC

EVEN THOUGH IT'S DAD'S TURN, I woke up wanting to be the one who's on watch. And now, I'm doing his shift and mine back to back, grateful to be spending Day Five, AEC, on the beach with the hulking FEMA containers far out of sight.

I started the morning by picking up where I left off on that illustration of the iceberg. Then, I switched to making diagrams of the changing patterns that shards of ice make when they bob and weave in the surf.

The sky's disconcerting shade of red-orange is back, spreading horizon to horizon even though it's only midday. Our local iceberg looks like it has a coal fire burning in its belly.

Last night, after Dad woke me and Stuart up from where we fell asleep on the grass and sent us to our respective bunks, I couldn't get back to sleep. Eyes closed tight in the dark, I listened to The Ollie's latest live mix. Its live soundtrack for the pre-dawn featured untamed creature moans, broken machine skreeks, and endless clawings and scratchings. I imagined it being the voice of a deranged storyteller recounting cryptic tales from the prehistoric future. I found that charming. That is how *not* charming the past four days have been.

The Ollie has continued gnarring in and out of my awareness ever since I came on watch. Maybe this is what our human habitat on planet Earth sounds and feels like, AEC. Maybe Ollie, Stuart and I are hearing-feeling the countless force fields that are erupting out of all the changings that are going on here on around us, and inside our own selves.

I take a long drink from my water bottle and look south to where Stuart, post-freerun, painfully makes his way up the entire length of the beach. He's dragging four or five bulging black garbage bags behind him through the sand.

As soon as he's within earshot, he calls out, "The zombie cruise ship must be breaking up. The far end of the beach is covered with vacation trash."

"Where did you get the garbage bags?"

"They washed up too."

At the foot of the beach stairs, he lets the bags drop and looks overhead. "It's noon, but the sky is so…"

"Orange?"

"Yeah," he says.

"The iceberg is breaking up the ship and the ship is breaking up the iceberg. See that rift just north of the bridge? It's new." I turn back to my sketchbook. "Everything is breaking up everything else."

Stuart sits in the sand next to me. I can tell he's watching me draw. I'm surprised at how much I don't mind him doing that.

We sit in silent conspiracy to not admit the reality of—yeah—everything we are looking at. Until…my eyes snap to the horizon.

"Hear that?" I ask.

"What, The Ollie?"

"That is not The Ollie," I say.

A jet ski careens around the northern point of the island and aims straight for our beach. The driver guns the motor. Stuart jumps up, grabs my arm, and pulls me out of the way. The machine runs aground a few feet from us.

It takes several seconds for me to realize that driver is the guy from town who came to check on us the other day. I didn't recognize him in his Coast Guard wet suit and helmet.

"That thing's some crazy shit," he shouts, nodding at the iceberg. He points to the official helmet on his head. "Me and my boatercycle here volunteered. I'm thinking I might go join up for real. They put you in training for three months. Then they send you out to do awesome stuff. Even crazier stuff than what they got me doing today." He pats the gear bag that he bungee-corded to his six pack. "They say three more icebergs showed up off New York City this morning. One of them is half the size of Long Island."

"What else is happening in New York?" I try not to sound as desperate as I am for his information.

"No riots, yet. Can't figure why not—their food's pretty much gone." He checks the bungee cords holding the six-pack. "Hey, how about this sky? Freaky. They say it's that color everywhere now. They can't figure out why *that's* happening either."

He laughs again as he fires up his jet ski, backs it into the water and lets it idle.

"Anyway, I thought NASA here might want to come with," he says, looking sideways at Stuart. "I'd let you help me put these Coast Guard antennas on that iceberg. And then, I'd let you help me drink these." He slaps the six-pack.

I flash a sarcastic roll of my eyes at Stuart. But when I catch the look on his face, my heart sinks. Is Stuart actually thinking of getting onboard with this guy?

The guy smirks and says, "Besides, those tourists had to leave *plenty* behind when they abandoned ship—know what I mean?"

"No," Stuart snaps.

"No, what?"

"No—I am not going to 'come with.'"

"Hey, whatever. But if either of you want to join up, I'll come get you off of here. You can reach me through the Captain."

He revs the jet ski and the exhaust blows Stuart's NASA cap into the churning wake.

I start after it, but Stuart catches my arm.

"Let it go," he says.

I'm seething as I watch the guy cowboy out to the iceberg and cut a slow lap around the cruise ship.

"I don't believe it," I say. "He wanted you to help him commit piracy. He must be drunk already. That ice bridge could come down on him any second."

As he watches the guy case the ship, Stuart's jaw tenses. I wouldn't be surprised if his hunger for a life of navigating twists and turns was gnawing at him. Any chance to get off

East Ledge Island—even if it takes joining the Coast Guard to do it—must be tempting.

"I wouldn't blame you for going out there with him. I mean, you know, for exploration's sake." Instantly, I hate my latest in doomed efforts to sympathize with Stuart over the demise of his NASA dream.

"He's not exploring. He's looting." Stuart turns his back on the whole scene, gathers up the unwieldy garbage bags, and drags them up the beach steps.

"We've got to figure out what to do with our trash," he says over his shoulder.

The mid-afternoon sky burns forest fire orange. Still on watch, I have been observing the would-be pirate manage— so far—to survive his mission of attaching antennas to outlying edges of the iceberg. The cracked and melting bridge is still intact. And, from what I can tell, the guy failed to figure out how to pillage a towering cruise ship from his tiny jet ski.

I amuse myself with the thought that, if he weren't working for the Coast Guard, he would qualify as an official sighting of, as Seaman Taylor put it, "unusual phenomena happening out there." In which case, I would be forced to report him.

I settle instead for the relief that comes from watching the ski jet, finally, careen away from the iceberg and disappear around the tip of East Ledge. It takes a while for my shoulders to relax.

Free of human prodding and poking, the iceberg seems less brittle and more like itself. The sounds of the surf return. The thick solitude of this island settles back in.

I listen for The Ollie. But if it's around, it's basking in the silence, too.

I head to the house for food.

Stuart was happy to take over my watch for an hour while I ate lunch, and even happier to return to the beach to cool off. He told me he moved trash management to the top of Dad's to-do list.

In the kitchen, Ollie and I make sandwiches with the last pack of cheese slices in Jennifer's stash. Everyone appears to be united in unspoken determination to delay taste testing FEMA's culinary skills for as long as possible.

Halfway through our respective sandwiches, Ollie and I agree that it is too hot at the picnic table to eat. We further agree that we should lower our body temperatures in the iceberg-cooled waters of the tidal pool.

So, we wrap our remaining lunch in napkins and set out to join Stuart at his watch post. On our way past the lighthouse, Ollie stops and gives the iceberg a long look of concern.

"Last night, I could smell it," she says. "It smelled like when a snow storm is coming."

She turns her back on the iceberg and kicks at the sandy path with her shoes.

"It's dying," she says. "We learned that in school, when there *was* school. We're killing everything."

I'm at a loss for what I should say back to the amazing ten-year-old next to me. This is only Day Five, AEC, but already, words we English-speaking humans have for talking about Ollie's unease—no longer fit. Coined in a different world, they are outdated leftovers from Earth, BEC.

Maybe there is nothing I *should* say back to Ollie, I tell myself. Maybe we haven't even begun to fathom what there is to say about—yeah—all the melting icebergs we are living with now. Maybe bending outmoded words so they *sort of* fit our strange new existence is the best we can offer.

"I don't think we're monsters, Ollie, but I'm not sure what we are."

"Will it ever get to be a glacier again?"

"Not for an awfully long time. But you know what? Time is one thing our iceberg has plenty of. So, sure, someday its melted water could find itself becoming a glacier again."

Ollie revives a bit.

"If you and Stuart are Generation Z, what am I? Nothing comes after Z."

Ollie has been harboring some serious questions.

"Of course, something comes after Generation Z," I say, trying to sound confident of that. "Let's see, after Generation Z comes—Generation 1.0. You are Generation 1.0, Ollie, because of the amazing new ways to live that you and your friends are going to invent and try out." I smooth her hair. "For starters, you have brand new clouds to spot. And you're going to learn so many new things from them."

"Yeah!" Ollie says, exuding fresh signs of life.

"Come on," I say. "Let's see if Stuart is keeping a proper watch."

We reach the top of the stairs and spot Stuart wading in the tidal pool below. He is not alone. He has unfurled the weather balloon across the surface of the pool and he's catching air in it.

"Hey Stuart! Whatcha' doing?" Ollie hollers.

Stuart looks up at us and takes a deep bow while gesturing "ta da!" with both arms. Then, he launches himself out of the water and belly flops onto the floating balloon.

Stuart has transformed NOAA's weather apparatus into a billowing raft with the dimensions of a small room. And he has assumed a lazy lounging position right in the middle of it.

"Awesome!" Ollie says under her breath.

"Hey, Ollie, I think Stuart needs to cool off after working so hard, don't you?"

A diabolical grin spreads across Ollie's face.

Skipping the stairs, we bound and squeal down the sandy cliff-side, plunge into the tidal pool on a full run, and scramble up onto the modified balloon craft.

Ollie trampolines into Stuart's arms, I grab his ankles, and, together, we send him tumbling, inelegantly, into the pool.

"Man overboard!" Ollie and I screech over and over.

For the first time, AEC, our beach echoes with uncontrollable laughter.

Flabby as a leaking waterbed, Stuart's balloon-raft undulates beneath our sprawled bodies. The three of us roll with the waves, doing nothing but watching clouds the color of orange Life Saver candies slide past overhead.

"Tomorrow, I'm going to rebuild the pier," Stuart says.

"Oh? So, you won't be joining the Coast Guard to escape

the confines of East Ledge via jet ski?" I intone. It's a feeble attempt to hide my surprise at how happy his announcement makes me.

"He's not what?" Ollie sounds alarmed.

Stuart laces his fingers behind his head and continues to cloud watch.

"I wanted to join NASA because I thought interplanetary space was the greatest course you could ever freerun," he says. "But, turns out, the ultimate freerunning course is right here. Complete with the most extreme obstacles we humans ever made for ourselves. With things changing this fast, pretty soon there won't be a planet more alien to us than this one. So, we might as well come to a landing on planet Earth—and figure out how to live on it."

Like I've been saying, tapped in.

"What are you guys talking about?" Ollie insists.

"We're going where no one has gone before, Ollie," Stuart pronounces.

"We are? Where!?"

But before we can even try to explain Earth, AEC to her, a grating, metallic rattle creeps into our awareness, quickly followed by—explosive popping sounds. We jostle into sitting up positions on the rippling balloon.

And that is when we see them—the small boats, a flotilla of them—rounding the southern tip of the island, their engines struggling against the swells.

"Those motors sound useless. They're barely making it," Stuart says. "I left the walkie talkie on the beach."

"I'll go get it," Ollie says. "We're supposed to call Seaman Taylor!" She scoots herself off the raft and starts to wade toward the beach.

"Ollie! Wait!" I call after her, but she keeps going. I turn to Stuart. "You want to turn them in?" I ask him in disbelief.

"We're supposed to. We're the blockade the Coast Guard couldn't put up."

"The people in those boats are only trying to get someplace safe. Just like everybody else is," I shoot back. "Just like my dad and I had to!"

The sound of straining motors cuts out.

Almost to shore, Ollie stops knee deep in the surf and points to the boats. "They're waving!" Ollie waves back.

"We've got to tell them to get away from here," I say, pushing off the balloon and sliding into the water. "They don't know what that iceberg could do to them!"

"Kally! Where are you going?" Stuart calls after me.

Ollie has reached the shore, and she's training the binoculars on the boats. "Somebody is getting in a raft," she shouts.

I splash my way up onto the beach and run to Ollie. Taking the binoculars, I bring the "somebody" she's talking about into focus.

"Oh, god." I drop the binoculars and stagger through the sand to *Home 2.0*. Then I drag her out into the tidal pool, pull myself onboard, and fumble with the sail.

"Kally! You can't go out there. You're the one who's always saying how dangerous it is." Stuart loses his balance and tumbles down onto the balloon. He struggles to all fours and shouts, "Kally, come on. *2.0* is not man-rated for open water."

I look right at him and yell across the pool, "That's my mom in that raft."

I don't blame Stuart for taking a moment to comprehend

what I just said. The instant he does, he rolls off the balloon, pushes through the knee-deep water, and—that vault he makes out of the pool and into *Home 2.0*? It would qualify him as half dolphin for sure.

I pilot *2.0* while Stuart trims her sail. Minutes after we clear the sandbar and enter open water, we're able to see my mom clearly. She is gripping the sides of her floundering raft. Except, it's not a raft at all. It's an inflatable toy. A yellow, polka dotted, sea monster toy.

Mom is soaked and looking our way. Her signature backpack drags heavy on her shoulders. The flotilla of overloaded boats chugs away from her, their motors backfiring and belching blue smoke.

I give Stuart the order to trim sail and we beat harder into the southerly wind. I am shouting "Mom!" over and over, and my heartbeat is more jagged than the flotilla's motors.

Mom struggles to wave to us as she clings to her sinking sea monster. She shouts and laughs my name a hundred times.

After what seems like hours, we are finally close enough to swing up into the wind and drift on our momentum into docking position. As we come alongside the limp inflatable, Stuart closes his hands around Mom's outstretched arms and pulls her into *Home 2.0*.

By now, Mom is breathing in gasps, beyond exhausted. We don't even say hello. Stuart and I need to focus on preventing our dangerously overloaded craft from swamping. I force *2.0* to come about. Then, I convince her to point toward shore. When I'm finally able to look out beyond the bow, I see Dad, bounding into the tidal pool.

My mind fails to save more than a few memories of our precarious sail back to East Ledge Island. Time speeds up. Dad and Mom are shouting each other's names. Dad is grabbing hold of our bow and pulling us through the tidal pool, then up onto the beach. When the three of us lock together in one endless, wet hug, I am shivering and laughing with more fear and joy than I thought any human could stand.

WHAT IS REAL

MOM HAS NOT REMOVED HER ARM from around my shoulders for what seems like hours. That is fine with me. And when it was Mom's turn to consider Jennifer's offer of that dry, pink tank top and those floral printed Capri pants, she said nothing could suit her better.

Dad and I have brought Mom up the lighthouse to introduce her to our local iceberg. I've never seen her so astonished. It'll take days and days to fill each other in on what we've learned about what's happening in the world, and inside our own selves. It will take at least one of those days to fully explain the four FEMA containers lined up and marching across the grounds below us. I don't think that Mom was tracking Ollie's fevered account earlier, the one about Ensign Brooks and the Civilian Emergency Corps. But, we are in no hurry to go there. There's too much gratitude to feel.

I float a wish over the iceberg and out to the horizon that

it obscures. "I hope it's OK that we never called the Coast Guard. I hope they made it," I say.

"They were from around here," Mom says, trying to sound reassuring. "They kept insisting they would be fine. They said they knew these waters really well. Their boats were in better shape than the freight trains I hopped between Boston and Portland, at least."

It is definitely too soon to hear *that* story. *Or* the one Dad and I could tell about the way that "knowing these waters well" became history on the Last Day, BEC. We'll talk about *that* soon enough, too.

For now, we three try to absorb the unfathomable fact that we are together, standing at the windows of a lighthouse, and watching an iceberg run aground on the underwater ledge of East Ledge Island—which we're living on.

"I hope Jennifer can help me send a thank you to Captain Vasquez. If her son had not walked across the Brooklyn Bridge and most of Manhattan to find me and tell me where you were…it could have been months before…what if I had gotten all the way home and you weren't…"

Mom's voice falters. She stands on tiptoes and kisses the top of my head. Dad kisses the top of hers.

Down on the grounds, a very busy Ollie with a very big logbook records readings from whatever weather instruments are still working.

"The Harts seem nice," Mom says.

"Stuart saved us," I say, not meaning to let it drop quite like that.

Her arm tenses around my shoulders and she reaches for Dad's hand. "Someday I'll let you two tell me that story."

After a second of silence, Dad says, "It's only right that the Harts get the house. This *is* their vacation."

Another second of silence, and we simultaneously burst into laughter at the absurdity of calling whatever this is a vacation.

"We'll be fine with anything." Mom says through gasps for air.

I touch the blue bracelet on her wrist and say, "I'm glad you still have this." I pretend I don't see the tears in her eyes.

"So am I." She squeezes my shoulders again. After another minute of iceberg-gazing, Mom says, "And, Stuart Hart. He seems to be very…"

She has been here for, what, all of three hours? And already, her nosy mom-self is fully operational and back online despite everything she's gone through.

"He seems to be very full of himself?" I suggest. "I know what you mean. I thought it was that, too. But really, it's his confidence. He's got lots of it. Probably because he has always known what it is that he wants to do with his life— until a few days ago."

"What happened then?" Mom asks.

"The future he has been dreaming of and training for forever got officially cancelled. He doesn't know what he'll be now that— Anyway, maybe he doesn't know *what* to be now, but for sure, he knows *how* to be."

Mom has that look she gets when she's trying to figure out what is going on with me. She could just come out and ask. But she won't. She thinks that would invade my privacy. What she doesn't get is that—right now? She could ask me anything. There is so much I want to talk to her about even if I don't know what any of it means.

Guessing that we women could use some time together, Dad clears his throat. "I'll go and get two FEMA cots out of the storage room. After dinner, we can set them up in the radio shack."

He kisses me on my forehead, touches Mom's arm, and disappears down the staircase.

"How long are we on watch?" Mom asks.

"Another hour."

She nods. We settle in as much as the stone and metal lantern room of this storm-battered lighthouse allows.

"I've been wanting to draw it from up here." I open my sketchbook and mom looks on as I start a new illustration of the iceberg.

"That's a big change from how you've been drawing," she says. "It's more…realistic."

"For days we've been looking at something so insanely unreal—I had to try to make it more real for myself. And maybe, for other people too."

Mom smiles. "I like this new sketchbook."

"Dad got it for me. To take on my college tour."

We get quiet. I guess we're having a moment of silence for my could-have-been college life. For *everyone's*.

Mom reaches into her pocket—make that, Jennifer's pocket—and pulls out a small sketchbook. It looks like it's been through a lot.

"I had this zippered inside my backpack the whole time. I got it last week, in the city, right before…anyway, it is dry at least, thanks to the disastrous miracle of shrink wrap." She shames the plastic with a scornful laugh. "I doubt that FEMA sent art supplies. So, you might be needing yet another sketchbook." She clears her throat. "It's for you," she says, and hands it to me.

I feel like I am holding a relic from a previous life—the one I lived on a different planet. I mean, seriously different, like the difference between the planet of the humans and the planet of the—yeah—whatever we are becoming, AEC.

"Your father and I seem to have realized the same thing at the same time," Mom says.

I pull myself back into the present. "And that would be?" I ask.

"It is time we stopped being afraid of your drawings."

"I know my drawings aren't real art like yours, but I didn't think they were frightening to anybody but me," I say, only half joking.

"I didn't mean it *that* way," Mom says, smiling. She turns to the window and examines the iceberg. "Your dad and I *were* afraid of your drawings, Kally. You felt something coming. But we didn't want to face it, and you were sensing *that* on top of everything else."

"Human antenna," I say.

Mom's eyebrow goes up.

"That's what Stuart calls me."

She waits for me to explain.

"Long story," I say.

"Which I look forward to hearing." Mom moves a few steps over to the next window. "Kally? Is that a *ship* out there under that ice—?"

"Another long story," I say.

She nods.

I start drawing again.

Mom does a complete circuit around the tower, checking

out all the views.

"Human antenna," I hear her say thoughtfully, as she rejoins me. "Stuart might have something there. *My* art has always come from what happens inside *here*," she taps her chest, "when I am alone in my studio. But *yours* comes from the connections that run between here," she taps my chest, "and everything else." She sweeps her arm across our 360-degree view.

We get quiet again. Then, she says, "I'm sorry, Kally. I'm sorry we haven't been brave, the way you are."

"But I'm *not* brave," I protest. "It's just that, what I saw happening around us and what I felt coming was nothing like they were telling us in school. Or on the news. Or in the movies, or—"

"Or at home."

"Yeah." I wish I could say otherwise.

"That's why you had to draw what you knew was real," Mom says.

I run my hand along the shrink-wrap of the book I'm holding. "At the orientation for the college tour I was supposed to go on next week, everybody was acting crazy," I say. "They couldn't stop talking about their dream futures and all the plans they had for making them come true. But— I *knew* that their futures were going to be nothing like their dreams." I look over at the iceberg. "I could never say so, though. They would think I was only being jealous because I couldn't come up with a dream of my own."

"It's not that you *couldn't*, Kally. It's just, part of you knew that all this was coming."

"Yeah, that part of me knew dream futures would be pointless."

"Having dreams for the future is never pointless," Mom says, "but the point of having them is going to be different from now on."

I look back at my mom and say, "I'm starting to think *I'm* not the strange stranger—the *world* is."

Mom steps away from the window and puts her arm around me again.

"Stuart said it."

"What did Stuart say?" she asks.

"We live on an alien planet now. It's awful and it's wonderful all at the same time. And—yeah—nobody knows what to do with that. It's not just me."

"No, it is not just you."

"There's no fixing it back to how it was, is there?"

"No. So, we will do the things we *can* do."

"I'm not quitting or anything like that. But—the planet is turning itself into something else—and we don't know what. I can't tell what I should do today or tomorrow, much less with my whole life."

Something on the beach catches Mom's attention. I follow her gaze to where Stuart has been hard at work, salvaging what's left of the storm-wrecked pier.

"You'll have no trouble seeing what needs doing, Kally. None of us will have to look further than our own fingertips to see what needs doing."

We watch Stuart uncoil a length of heavy-duty marine rope, and I explain, "Stuart is making us a breakaway pier."

"There *is* such a thing?"

"He's inventing it right now, out of inflatable lifeboats, compliments of FEMA. He's designing it to break away in the next big storm and float with the force fields. Then, we'll salvage what we can and use it to invent the next pier." I smile at the thought and say, "Falling and landing."

"Falling and landing?" Mom asks.

Once again, she can't understand what I'm talking about, and she looks worried about that—which makes me laugh.

"Yeah, they're the same thing. I'll show you sometime."

I spot Dad on the grounds outside the keeper's house. He's eyeing up the emptied FEMA containers. It wouldn't surprise me if he's making plans to turn them into something that he knows we are going to need.

"So, about you and Dad…," I venture.

Mom watches Dad for a few moments, then says, "We're falling. And we're landing."

DAY SIX, AEC

THE SUNRISE STAINS THE ICEBERG, and me, the colors of mixed fruit sorbet. Quickly, the cloudless morning sky settles into its new and disturbing day-long orange phase, just like it did yesterday.

It was Dad's turn to be on watch last night. He and Mom camped out on the top deck of the lighthouse. Mom couldn't pull herself away from him, nor the aerial view of our iceberg.

They might be asleep, so I tread as quietly as possible up the metal spiral. Halfway to the top, I hear their drowsy chatting.

Dad's morning voice: "You know that sound I told you Kally's been hearing? I finally heard it too—just before you woke up. Whatever is making it, it must have gotten closer—or stronger."

I stop on the stairs and savor the soft echoes of their voices.

"Are you sure we should let her go out in the new boat you made? It's tiny. And that iceberg, David. No, she shouldn't go out there."

"'Out there' is all around them. It's where they went to rescue you. It's where they sleep, and draw, and run. They live there now. But, last night, I did tell Kally she should stay inside the tidal pool from now on."

Silence.

Mom's voice: "This is going to be hard, isn't it?"

They need time to talk. I back my way down the stairs on tiptoe. At the bottom rung, I literally bump into Stuart.

"Let's go for a sunrise sail," he proposes cheerily.

I put my finger to his lips and turn him toward the door.

I look up at the lighthouse. Dad and Mom are at the windows, arms around each other's waists. Stuart freeruns down the stairs as I wave up to the tower. The wave my mom sends back is big enough to count as rogue.

Minutes later, I'm in the helm seat, watching Stuart work *Home 2.0*'s crazy quilt of a patched-up sail. His technique is becoming downright seafaring.

The tidal pool beneath us reflects the brilliant orange sky above us, enveloping us in an unworldly atmosphere that turns Stuart's face the color of burnished copper.

"We could be on Mars!" I say, laughing.

I can't believe I said that, and I swallow my laughter. For one thing, we are on a planet that should be blue, not red. For another, no human will ever be on Mars—there won't be a human-piloted 2045 mission for Stuart to flight control. And so, yet again, I find myself wishing I could take back something I've said to Stuart.

Our silence is painful, and I'm relieved when Stuart finally breaks it.

"You had the right idea, you know," he says, squinting at the iceberg.

"What idea was that?" I ask, trying to get past my embarrassment.

"Earth is enough."

"I don't remember saying anything like—"

"Your drawings say it."

The wind shifts, bringing me to attention in my seat. "Ready to come about," I say.

We pilot *Home 2.0* into a lazy turn and Stuart resets the sail.

"Not only were you right, you know, that Earth is enough. This whole time, *you* were the only one who was on course for their future."

"I know it's getting hard to remember life, BEC, but I clearly remember *never* being that person."

"Kally, listen." It sounds like Stuart is preparing to talk matters of life and death again. "I thought I was on course to be a flight controller. But you can't be a flight controller without a flight plan, and there are no flight plans for where life on this planet is heading. We don't need flight controllers—we need what you've known how to do all along."

"I don't think I follow—"

"You wanted the lines you draw in your sketchbooks to be your flight plan. You wanted them to show you the path to your life's calling. But they could never do that. You know why? Because you are *already* living your life's calling."

"Really. And that would be…?"

"Wayfinding."

"Wayfinding, you say."

"That's right. The ancient art of finding your way as you go. It's the one thing that has a chance of keeping you from getting lost when nobody has a map. Those lines you make in your sketchbook are *you*, laying down your flight path as you go."

I lean back in the helm seat to consider Stuart's take on what it is he thinks I "do."

"Wayfinder," I repeat, trying it on for size. "It's got a better ring to it than *human antenna*, I'll give it that."

Stuart laughs and says, "Maybe so, but they're both part of the course."

Right then, The Ollie decides to speak up.

"Do you hear that?" I ask.

"Who could miss it?" Stuart says.

We swivel our heads, trying to zero in on the emphatic vibrations. This time, I believe we might be able to trace the path of the sound waves to their origin…

which is…

somewhere near…

no…

the voice is coming *exactly* from…

"The iceberg!" I shout and crack up with laughter. "Stuart! The Ollie is the *iceberg*!"

When I look across *2.0* at Stuart, he has turned to face the iceberg and he is beaming rays of one hundred percent, pure curiosity at it.

"Let's go see what planet we've landed on," he says.

I choke back my giddy delight as every cautionary tale

my sailor dad told me starts to flash before my eyes. So does Dad's new rule about not leaving the tidal pool. But then, so do Stuart's tales about how Earth is enough, and how there are no flight plans, and—yeah—how we'll need to wayfind as we go if we don't want to get lost in life, AEC.

I sit at the helm, tiller in hand, not knowing which direction to point *Home 2.0*. I am in irons again, tangled in the signals and scrambled forces that are pouring in. But, as the knot in my chest tightens, it forces the realization that, worst of all, I am tangled in *fears*.

A flash of intuition sparks. It speaks in full sentences: *You can't find your way as you go if you're afraid of the going.*

Afraid of the going—I've been *afraid of the going*. I've been drawing Earth's new forces fields, all right—and one of them is the mangled knot of my own fear. Fear of going on that college tour without a map to steer by. Fear of having to find my dream as I go.

Stuart turns away from the iceberg to see why I have fallen silent. I look from the excitement in his face, out across the ocean, to the iceberg's aloofness. My mind races as it struggles to gauge distance, wind, surf. But that only makes what Stuart said more obvious: there are no gauges or flight plans for what we are about to do. We will have to find our way as we go.

Reaching into the leg pocket of my sailing pants, I dig out Stuart's NASA cap.

"This washed up on the beach yesterday," I say. I try to smooth its creases, give up, and hold it out to him.

Stuart hesitates, but only for a second.

He takes the cap and runs his fingers along its logo. Then, he leans across *Home 2.0* and places it on my head. I grip the visor and seat it firmly over my hair.

Giving the signal: "Bearing away," I reset *2.0*'s sail for the mouth of the tidal pool. Confusions, unmanageable force fields, unknowable futures, fears about the going. They're all right here, coming right along with us. But, at this moment at least, the fact that it couldn't be otherwise feels slightly more livable.

As we enter the open sea, I don't look back at the lighthouse windows.

The iceberg grows nearer, larger, and more real until—it is flat-out incomprehensible. Even the ridiculous cruise ship fails to blunt its wildness.

"Being with it like this, instead of denying it or fearing it—it makes what is happening—"

"—a little more real?" Stuart offers.

"Yes. Yes," I say.

"In a good way?" Stuart asks.

Now, there's a question. I don't have an answer, but I have a story Stuart once told me. And I say, "Good in the way it is when you manage to surf an unstoppable wave—and then get to make something of where it takes you."

As we close in on its western edge, we can actually see the iceberg stress and crack. It is sloughing off millions of bits of itself every second.

Beneath us, an invisible, inverted mountain of ice grates against the underwater shelf of East Ledge, scouring and grooving it mercilessly. Waves of sound rise through the water. *Home 2.0*'s aluminum hull resonates with the tortured grindings. From far above us, squeals and pops rain down as the iceberg's massive surfaces of time and cold break and form, break and form.

Turning into the wind on a course that takes us toward the southern spires, we wayfind a precarious path for *Home 2.0* through frigid down drafts, hot updrafts, and violent shudders.

As we reach the closest approach we dare to make, the iceberg's voice intensifies into a visceral mashup of crushing sea floor, gasping air holes and twisting moans. Above it all, we hear high-pitched hissing sounds—like seltzer—as air escapes from the melting ice.

"Cryptic tales from a prehistoric future," I say.

Stuart looks at me, puzzled.

"The iceberg *has* been talking to us."

"What is it saying?" Stuart asks.

"I'm not sure. But I'm going to listen."

We round the southern tip and run with the wind up the far side.

That is when I hear, or maybe I feel, something else. Something *other.* I clutch the tiller with both hands, turn my head to starboard, and discover that—it's happening again. There, on the horizon, hidden until now by the massive body of our iceberg—a second one. A monstrous one. The mountains of this emerald green newcomer are glacial, soaring at least ten times the height of those beside us. Fog clouds trail from its peaks—ghostly flags of a phantom ship that has been on its way to East Ledge since the last ice age.

I let go of the tiller.

Alarmed, Stuart pivots in his seat to follow my gaze. The line to the boom slips from his hand. *Home 2.0*'s sail goes slack.

Our fellow travelers take hold of us in their tremendous force fields—altering our course—as we alter theirs.

I turn and see Stuart greeting this new arrival with a smile of overflowing astonishment. Without taking his eyes away from the icebergs, he reaches his hand out to me.

I lean across the tiller and close my hand around his.

It's not romantic. At least, not in any BEC kind of way. It is way more than that. It's two humans giving each other a foothold in the maelstrom of change that their habitat has become.

DAY FOURTEEN, AEC

IT HAS BEEN SEVEN DAYS SINCE Stuart and I defied the rules of sane seamanship and set sail to meet our local iceberg. Seven days since we sailed into the even stranger world that met us on its other side. Since then, Earth and its humans have continued to live out one outlandish surge of transformation after another.

At first, I tried to make myself write it all down. But when I stopped trusting that—you know—there would be another day, I saw no point in keeping a daily journal. That would be so BEC.

Besides, we've been busy.

Jennifer has made at least two dozen friends on the radio so far. She helps them relay calls for assistance and messages about missing persons.

These days, much of the local weather is being brought

to us by the new iceberg. That's why, when a Coast Guard helicopter did a flyover and parachuted a special delivery from Ensign Brooks, it had Ollie's name on it. And now, *Home 2.0* and I take Ollie and her new weather instrument out beyond the sandbar twice a day. She measures iceberg-modified air and water conditions, and walkie talkies the data back to Chief Forecaster Williams. The Coast Guard has no idea where the new iceberg is headed. The Gulf Stream in the Atlantic is changing too much and too fast.

Mark asked me to talk to him tonight about the drawings I was making, BEC. He's been working on ways to track complex pattern changes and phase shifts.

Mom is getting creative with the FEMA food, but there is only so much a person can do. She's been studying a book she found on the bookshelf. It's a field guide to the edible seaweed around here. Before we eat any, though, we need to confirm with the Coast Guard that it still is edible. She and Jennifer have bonded over the fishing gear we found in the storeroom, even though they never fished in their lives. They can't wait to give surf fishing a shot tomorrow morning.

And, three days ago, Dad, Mom, and I started to convert the three empty FEMA containers into lodging. Grid refugees in highly unseaworthy DIY craft have been threading their ways north past the icebergs and growlers off our island. Dad says it will not be long before the events of AEC force one or more of them to put in here. So, between our watches, we each crewed for Stuart and got his breakaway pier constructed in two days flat. Now, he's networking the couple of dozen portable solar panels from FEMA into one big one. Which means that we'll be able to turn off the annoying, smelly generator.

I'm in charge of outfitting East Ledge Island's new container cabins and I have been forced to perform multiple acts of emergency interior decoration already. I get to glamp out in the blue container tonight. Mom and Dad will move into the yellow one when it's ready. We're preparing the white one—along with half a dozen FEMA cabin tents— for when people might be forced to shelter here.

Despite my doubts, then, days *have* kept coming. So, I changed my mind and decided I would write this all down after all. This past week, I grew muscles in my fingers from pounding out these pages. The typewriter Stuart and I resurrected from the radio shack's storeroom has an attitude.

Based on the past seven days then, I have begun to believe that not only *will* more days come—they *should*. Because, while the terrible things of each new day, AEC, are fully and tragically real, the wondrous things are every bit as real, too.

Tomorrow, I'm starting a field journal in the sketchbook that Mom carried here through so many breakings and formings. Each day I will draw what's real—at the moment. Then, when the next day comes and rearranges all our footholds and handholds again, I'll draw what's real—at *that* moment.

And—yeah—that's how I'll find my way, as I go.

DAY FIFTEEN, AEC

Stuart and I listened to the icebergs today.
What they're saying changes everything.
Even if we have to invent a whole new way of drawing, we're going to draw that.

ABOUT THE AUTHOR

Solid Broken Changing is Elizabeth Ellsworth's first Young Adult novel. It is inspired by her experiences of co-existence on planet Earth as an educator, writer, and collaborative artist. With Jamie Kruse, she co-directs smudge studio (smudgestudio.org), based in Brooklyn, NY and Provincetown, MA. Their projects connect daily life experiences to vast, generative forces of geological and cosmological change. The story of *Solid Broken Changing* grew out of their work as artists living the Anthropocene.

www.ingramcontent.com/pod-product-compliance
Lightning Source LLC
Chambersburg PA
CBHW030740110726
47900CB00008B/2386